Can You Speak Feline?

Can You Speak Feline?

Rose Henry

Text copyright © 2023, Rose Henry

Book Cover Design copyright © 2023, Rose Henry

All rights reserved

For Steve, Amy and Evie,
and the many cats and dogs, past and present,
who have graced our lives.

Chapter One

I heard two people on the other side of the wooden garden fence. It's past midnight, an odd time to be gardening, but at least they are being polite, whispering to each other.

I've been sat for a while waiting for the rain to stop, beneath the leafy laurel bush at the bottom of Esther Dickie's garden, to continue my Patrol. I like the way the rain enhances the scent of the laurel leaves, and the plants probably welcome the rain, but I don't like getting wet.

The wiggle in my whiskers, my early warning radar, is the first sign the two people behind the fence are not doing a spot of gardening. A pair of size nine, muddy trainers with frayed grey laces land with a thump four feet away from me. They were followed by a pair of black boots, size twelve, also muddy and scuffed badly at the toes. From the state of them, the boots haven't seen a duster, or a tin of polish, since the day they were made. I admit, I am an expert when it comes to shoes, at twelve inches tall, it's the first thing in my line of vision when meeting people, or uprights, as we felines call you.

I look up from the trainers. He's a very young man, or an older boy. He's short and quite reedy. He'd benefit from a few good meals from Anna to put some meat onto his bones. He's wearing tight jeans, ripped at the knees, a black hoody and a large saggy grey rucksack hangs from his back. Boots is much older, taller and stocky, all in black, from the boots to his woolly hat, which he has pulled low, covering his eyebrows.

'See that window to the left of the back door?' Boots whispers pointing at Esther's cottage.

'Uh ha' Trainers said, nodding.

'Well, its loose; that's our way in. We need to jimmy the lock; give me the palette knife.'

Trainers dropped to his knees and swung the ruck sack from his shoulder onto the ground in front of me. I stay still and watch him ferret around in the bag. His face is thin and gaunt; he has the look of a rat with small quick furtive eyes. He twists his lips into a thin line as he hands Boots what looks like an icing knife, with a bendy blade and a round edge. I've seen Anna use this implement when trying to ice cakes. She may be a brilliant artist but her skill with paint on canvass doesn't translate to icing cakes.

Trainers whispered harshly 'What's that?' and points at me.

Boots took a stride towards Trainers, bends with his hands on his knees and stares at me.

I didn't move, after all, I was here first.

'It's just a moggie' Boots said dismissively and stood up.

How very rude, just a moggie, I'm a jet black British Shorthaired and proud of it!

'I hate cats and I don't like the way it's looking at me' Trainers said as he stood up and swung one of his tatty trainers at me.

I dodged the trainer and sprang out into the open, arching my back, legs locked stiff, making myself taller.

'Oh come on, leave it alone, we've got work to do' Boots said.

'Yeah, you're right, go on, out of it!' Trainers sneered as he swung his right hand at me.

I defended myself, hissing and lashed out with a FCA - Full Claw Attack – which feline law permits when threatened or hunting. I jabbed him across the back of his hand twice. It was a good hit; I rarely miss.

'You little rat!' Trainers hissed and sucked his hand.

Boots chuckled and said 'Leave it alone. You deserved that, now come on, time is ticking, we don't have all night.'

Trainers glared at me whilst still sucking the trickle of blood from his hand and I stared back. He blinked first; uprights always do.

'I still don't like the way it's looking at me, it's a knowing one, it's seen us' Trainers said.

Boots shrugged and shaking his head said 'Does it matter? What's it going to do, tell the coppers? Come on.'

Trainers sniffed and hoisting his bag over his shoulder, silently followed Boots over the lawn to the back of Esther's cottage. I walked back beneath the laurel bush and swung right following them, walking briskly beneath the vegetation dripping with water which made me shudder. I hid behind some large empty planters that were stacked ready for Esther to fill with plants in the spring.

I watched Boots use the palette knife against the window frame, jiggling it up and down until I heard a click. He opened the window enough to put his fingers beneath the frame and handed the palette knife back to Trainers. Using both hands, he slowly pushed the sash window upwards. Boots stared inside; it was dark in there. I knew they were looking into the kitchen and below the window was the sink. Boots heaved himself upwards and climbed in. Trainers wound a grubby piece of cloth around his hand which I noted with some pride was still trickling with blood. He looked behind him briefly and then hoisted himself up through the window and followed Boots. I heard another click and saw a torch light dance across the wall.

House breakers! Not that Esther's house is broken, but Boots and Trainers aren't here for a saucer of milk or a tin of pilchards, they are here uninvited to take things, or worse, to hurt Esther.

I sprung over the pots and leaped onto the window ledge and followed them in. I don't need a torch; I have night vision. I tracked muddy footprints across the kitchen, into the hall and turned left into the front sitting room. The bag was on the carpet looking floppier than it had before. Boots was lifting Esther's old clock with a wooden polished casement and a painted face. The clock ticked loudly and Esther wound it every day with an ornate key. I watched in disbelief as he wrapped it carefully in a grubby looking towel.

Trainers torch light swung from the clock and around the room. The light caught a photo of Esther's late husband, George, which sat in a silver frame on the highly polished side board next to an art deco bronze statue of a slim dancing lady. Trainers picked up the bag and moved over to the side board and started to load the frame and statue into the bag.

I had to do something! I don't understand why uprights like things, but these things are important to Esther. I've often found Esther talking to George's photo when I've wandered in to check up on her. She's told me many times how George had saved every penny he'd earnt to buy her the statue as his wedding present to her. The clock was her own Mothers, who'd had it for years before giving it to Esther, so I know it was very old, as Esther's old herself.

As Trainers was reaching for six tiny crystal swans, I lept onto the side board, hissing which startled Trainers. I saw his eyes widen and I took advantage, striking at his hand reaching for the crystal figures. Trainers cried out and dropped the bag with a bang. He lunged towards me and missed. I jumped onto the small side table next to Esther's favourite armchair. He swung around after me and I dodged him with ease. Really, does he think he can out reflex me? He lost balance and fell heavily against the table which rocked and fell with a thud.

'What the hell are you doing, you oaf!' Boots whispered harshly.

'That cat; it's in here!' hissed Trainers.

We all heard the noise from upstairs; Esther was out of bed.

I watched Boots look around quickly; he pointed to the six crystal swans and whispered harshly 'Take those, we don't have time for anything else.'

Trainers pushed the crystal swans into his pockets and picking up his bag, followed Boots out of the room.

The light from the landing was on upstairs, casting a glow midway down the stairs and I could hear Esther moving around slowly.

'Let's go' Boots whispered.

I followed them back to the kitchen and watched as Boots hurriedly clambered out and took the clock swaddled in his towel which Trainers handed back to him. Trainers climbed out with the rucksack on his back.

I jumped onto the window sill and watched as they disappeared to the bottom of the garden. I was torn; should I follow them or stay and look after Esther? Esther is very old, and she only has one life.

The kitchen light was turned on and I turned and blinked at Esther. She has her pink fluffy dressing gown on which is inside out with the seams showing, and far too big for her with the sleeves covering her hands. Her grey hair hung beside her face and I'm surprised to see how long it has grown. She usually wears it in a bun with a couple of pencils, art brushes or anything long and thin stuck in it. Her hair swayed as she walked towards me. As always, she smelt of lavender but looked tired and sleepy.

'Claude, what are you doing here, it's a bit early for …' she stopped and blinked as she saw the open window. Her eyes widened as she noticed the muddy scuff marks on the window sill and in the sink. She turned without a word and I followed her as she traced the muddy footprints into her sitting room. She switched on the light and leaning against the door frame groaned, shaking her head. She seemed to shuffle to her arm chair and sat down heavily. She sagged into herself, her usual soft pink cheeks had lost their colour and she closed her eyes and sighed.

I leaped onto the arm of her armchair and then onto her lap.

She gave no response.

I started to pummel her legs with soft paws and began to purr, a sound I've found that most uprights find comforting. That seemed to do the trick, and she looked down at me with eyes swimming with water; she looked so sad.

'Thank you Claude' she whispered as she lifted her hand and stroked my back.

'Not at all' I said. She doesn't understand me; she doesn't speak feline.

Esther reached for her telephone on the window sill and called 999.

I stayed until the police arrived. They seemed to be nice uprights with well-made solid polished boots and chunky belts with all sorts of things attached. One of the police officers was a young woman who made Esther a sweet cup of tea. I knew she was in safe hands, this beverage seemed to resolve all problems, as far as I can tell.

There was nothing more I could do. Esther was safe and sitting with a large tea pot in front of her, talking to the police officer. I headed home for breakfast.

Chapter Two

The pet entrance at home is at the back of the house and leads directly into a large warm kitchen diner which always smells of freshly brewed coffee and warm bread.   As soon as I stepped in, the door banging behind me, I was ambushed by Connie, a bouncy four-year golden Cocker Spaniel, with long silky ears and domed shaped head.

Connie should know better than pounce at me as soon as I come home, something she hasn't done since her puppy age.

She barked 'at last' and sank to the floor. She put her front feet forward, lay her head on them and looked at me with large soft brown eyes. The big clue that something was wrong was her tail; it was still.

I stepped towards her and touched her nose with mine. It's not something I do a lot with canines but Connie's part of my family. I've taught Connie basic feline, and I understand elements of the canine language but, as a cat, it's a devil of a job to speak it. I asked her what was wrong.

'It's Vincent!' Connie howled 'He's not here, and hasn't been in all night.'

My fur prickled with alarm, a bit like the hairs on your arms standing on end. Vincent is another cat who is part of our family. He joined us as a tiny kitten, from a nearby rescue sanctuary eight months ago. When Anna and Alex bought him home, he bolted beneath the sofa in the sitting room as soon as he was released from the cat carrier. He wouldn't come out, despite appeals and reassurance from me, Anna and Alex. He thought Connie was an alien with her long floppy ears and ear-shattering bark. Anna resorted to making him a bed from a shoe box stuffed with a small jumper which she put under the sofa. She put a cat litter tray next to the sofa for his comfort. Food and water were served in bowls under the sofa, which Anna slowly drew out each meal time until they got to the edge. The little chap was doing well, and was finally settling in until he met the rug in front of the fire place. The rug is woollen and fluffy and it sent him scurrying for safety under the sofa again. He spent his days watching the rug for movement. His mind was eventually taken off the rug, and he even bonded with Connie via drastic measures; ping pong balls. Anna bought a sack full and they were everywhere, still are, if you know where to look. Connie preserved some for safe keeping in the garden but most huddle under the sofa, crowding together with ideas that they are perhaps safer in numbers?

To this day, Vincent walks around the rug which he considers evil without telling us why. He shakes his head at me in total disbelief when I assure him that it won't hurt him. He constantly warns Connie that no good will come if she continues to lie on it.

Vincent has grown out of kittenhood but not reached his first birthday and old enough to join the Cadets. He's at the stage of exploration and has already fallen in next doors fish pond, fell out of numerous windows at various heights and had a go at climbing a ladder, even though it was occupied by a male upright clinging on for dear life as Vincent played with his shoelaces. He's quite small for his age but growing into his fur which is ginger and faintly striped. His paws, whiskers and face are white with ginger falling down the centre of his face which makes him look like he has a mask on.

I tried to sound positive and said 'I'm sure he's fine and out somewhere with Mabel.' Mabel is next door's cat, and Vincent's best friend.

'No, Mabel's home, her uprights locked her in last night, she wouldn't tell me why when I saw her this morning' Connie said.

'Oh Claude! Thank goodness you're here' Anna said hurrying towards me. She's slim, quite tall and has her size six soft leather indoor moccasins on. She bent down and picked me up. Anna and Alex are the only ones I will allow to do this. I gave her a mini purr; to be fair I am all purred out looking after Esther, but my head snuggled under her chin. She put me down, gently ruffled Connie's head, opened the kitchen door and bellowed 'Vincent!, Vincent!' and stood peering into the garden with her arms folded.

Alex popped his head from the doorway which leads into the village shop they own and said 'Stop fretting Anna, look Claude's back, he's been out all night and perfectly fine, aren't you boy?'

I nodded.

'Claude is old enough to look after himself, Vincent's a wee bit too small' Anna said.

'You won't be saying that when he brings home a mouse. That's probably what he's doing, you'll see.' Alex said as his head disappeared from the doorway, and I could hear him talking to a customer.

Anna sighed, and after peering into the garden again, although it is still dark and she doesn't have night vision, she slowly shut the door. She looked down at us and said one of my favourite words, 'Breakfast.'

I watched her produce our bowls from a cupboard and food from another. She hesitated over the bowl for Vincent, but filled it and put them all down on the floor with another bowl of fresh water; the only kind of water I'll tolerate.

Alex's head appeared again and he said 'Hey, there are police cars outside Esther's house.'

Anna blinked 'The police? I hope she's alright, I'll pop round later.'

'Mmm yes okay, I'll get off to the wholesalers early and get back' Alex said.

'Okay, give me a minute and I'll be in as soon as I've made a coffee.'

I watched Anna click the kettle on, a horrible thing that produces steam, and when the water is bubbling, gives out a shrill whistle. She glanced down at us and said 'Not hungry, worried about Vincent too?'

I didn't answer, Anna's great but doesn't speak feline either.

As soon as she'd made her coffee, (should be tea) I turned to Connie and said 'Ready? You need to use your nose.'

Connie nodded eagerly, stood up, her long ears swirling and sprung through the pet door. I followed and sat on the patio with my tail curled around my feet. I watched Connie, her nose to the ground, wander over our very long and large lawn and along the borders, working her way down the garden. At the rear fence, she shouted 'Here!'

I ran to her and she said with small yelps and whimpers 'The strongest scent is here.'

I nodded, jumped onto the fence, and balanced on the top. Connie looked up at me and said 'See anything?'

'I can see lots of things but not what we are looking for.'

'There's no need to be sarcastic, we're all worried about Vincent' Connie snapped.

'Just a minute' Mr Featherstone's buckets are not stacked but scattered.'

'It's hardly the time to be judgemental about untidy buckets' Connie said.

'I'm never judgemental' I said.

'Hmmff!' Connie snorted.

Mr Featherstone is a cleaner of anything outdoorsy from windows to cars and bikes of all descriptions. He takes his work very seriously and has colour coded buckets for every type of job. He is a very tidy person, even the plants in his garden are arranged in an orderly fashion without a leaf out of place. I admit, it wasn't much to go on, but my whiskers twitched.

'I won't be long' I said and walked along the back fence, turning to walk along the side fence into Mr Featherstone's garden. Fence walking is an excellent way to have a good aerial view. I'm surprised uprights don't do it, although to be fair, balancing along a two-inch wide, six-foot high fence isn't something you would naturally do. You do make up for your lack of balance with something far more useful; thumbs.

I stepped onto the roof of Mr Featherstone's shed which stands by the side fence and shimmied down the wall, landing amongst the buckets which were mostly on their sides. I looked inside them but they were all empty. I looked up at the shed, the door was closed. If Vincent was in there, it would be a big job to bust him out. I jumped onto the tarpaulin which covered Mr Featherstone's motor bike and peered into the shed window. I couldn't see anything other than gardening tools and shook my head. No, Vincent may be young, but he wasn't stupid enough to be trapped in a shed, and yet my whiskers where really wiggling now; I knew I was close.

I'm not one to rush around like a box of bees and sat on the tarpaulin to think. I caught the sound of a tiny whimper. I pricked my ears forward and heard the sound again; it was coming from beneath me. I jumped onto the ground and edged under the tarpaulin. It was very dark but, as I think I've mentioned, that's never been an issue.

Two deep green eyes in a small white face blinked at me from behind the front tyre. I could smell blood and oil and inched closer. It was Vincent. His ear was torn, he had blood on his shoulder and oil on his back. He didn't move but his small body trembled.

I got closer to him, edging slowly and touched his nose with mine.

He blinked at me again and I could see a film half covering his eyes. I recognised the signs; he was in shock.

'What happened?' I whispered.

Vincent stared at me.

'It's me, Claude, what happened?' I said again.

'Retro' Vincent whispered as if that explained it all, and it did.

Retro the cat. Kittens are warned by their mothers that Retro will bite and steal their tails if they don't behave. I've never been a fan of such nonsense, but Retro is a bully and an ambusher of kittenhood along with his crew, the V-C's.

It occurred to me Vincent has never seen Retro but he seems very certain it was. Retro's been out of the area for a while along with his leader, Vixen. Now is not the time to ask Vincent any more questions; I need to get him home.

'Can you walk?' I asked.

Vincent stared and blinked at me.

I touched his nose again with mine and repeated 'Can you walk?'

Vincent nodded.

'Come on, let's go home' I said.

'Retro?'

'You are quite safe with me' I said.

He gave a tiny nod and stood. Pain flittered across his face.

'Come on, nice and slow.'

I pushed through the tarpaulin and had a good look around as Vincent slowly came out and stood next to me. I looked at his wound on his shoulder which was seeping blood. I knew Vincent wouldn't have the energy to jump up on the fence and balance along it, so I slowly guided him across the garden, using the shortest route possible to the rear fence. I left him briefly sitting next to a gnome with a green hat and a cheerful face and jumped onto the fence. Connie was sat where I left her. She looked up anxiously and said 'Have you found him?'

'Yes, but he's been hurt by Retro. Can you dig under the fence?'

She didn't ask questions, possibly had the same questions I have about Retro, but started to scrabble at the mud under the fence with her front paws, moving the earth away with her back ones.

I jumped down next to Vincent who was shivering violently and watched as a gap appeared beneath the fence. When the gap was big enough, I shouted to Connie 'Coming through' and pushed my head against Vincent's little body to urge him forward. He crawled through slowly and when his tail had finally disappeared, I jumped the fence again and landed on the other side next to Connie.

Our garden is very long and Vincent was in no shape to make it to the pet door. I'd usually pick him up by the scruff of his neck but the position of his wound stopped me; it would hurt him. I needed to think how to get him there. Connie must have also felt Vincent was not able to trek to the house either. If this had been any other canine, I'd have clawed its eyes out, but I trust Connie and watched her pick Vincent up with a soft mouth. With her head high, she trotted up the garden and I jogged alongside her. Vincent's eyes were closed and his head lolled gently.

Connie surged through the pet door and I followed. She gently lay Vincent down and sprinted through the kitchen to the connecting door to the shop. She barked sharply and incessantly.

Connie ran back to Vincent as Anna emerged from the shop and said 'What is it girl; what's all the noise? You'll scare the customers away and ...' Anna stopped and stared at Vincent lying between us.

He was very still, his eyes closed and blood was coating his fur a sticky deep red.

Anna rushed forward, dropped to her knees and stroked Vincent gently. 'He's alive' she whispered, relief in her voice.

I nodded and Connie barked once.

She pulled her mobile phone from a pocket in her jeans and stabbed at it – the Vets. I don't like the Vets; they aren't very polite uprights, always sticking things up one's bottom or jabbing needles that are never asked for, but even I knew that a Vet was someone Vincent needed now. I heard her say 'Yes, I'll bring him in straight away.'

Anna got up and disappeared through the door to the shop. I heard keys rattling in the front shop door as she locked it. She appeared again, briefly, talking into her phone, and disappeared upstairs. Moments later she reappeared carrying a clean white towel. She picked

Vincent up gently and swaddled him in the towel before lifting him. Grabbing her keys from the key pot by the front door to the house, she left, the door slamming behind her. She's still wearing her indoor moccasins.

Chapter Three

Connie and I looked at each other and then at breakfast. I had no appetite; my stomach had knotted itself up. I paced through the kitchen into the hall, walked past the inner door to the shop, and swung right into the sitting room at the front of the house. Connie followed; her breakfast untouched too. She slumped onto the rug. I jumped onto the sofa, which sits under the window, and lay sphinx like on the top of it where I have a good view of the road.

Our home is a detached house which has two doors to the front, one leads into the shop which sells newspapers, magazines, sweets, tobacco, wines, soft drinks, homemade cakes (un-iced), dairy products, groceries, and stationery. The shelves are stacked full with military precision. Huge low freezers sit in the centre of the shop containing ice-cream and frozen foods, including my favourite fish dishes.

The shop is the only one in the village and is always busy. People pop in going to or leaving work in the nearby business parks and city. The village has an infant and junior school where children go from the sprawling housing estate built at the edge of the village. The children buy sweets, comics, pens, pencils and paper and bring a lot of noise and laughter. They sometimes see Connie and I through the pet gate and ask Alex if they can stroke Connie. I know Connie loves the attention and sometimes lies on her back to allow them to rub her tummy. Older people, like Esther, pop in most days for milk, groceries and a chat.

The door between the house and the shop is always open but has a pet gate in the doorway. Anna and Alex think this will prevent us thumbless beings from going into the shop. That may be true for Connie but it wouldn't be a problem for me. I leave Anna and Alex believing the pet gate is effective and spend many hours lying on the floor just by it and watch people come in. From this position, I've been able to make an extensive study of shoes.

One police people carrier is still parked outside Esther's house, which is four houses down the hill from ours; Esther must need a lot of tea. I watch large, medium, and small people carriers pull up, uprights get out of them and walk to the shop door, try the handle to get in, peer in and then walk away. I see Ida Morris coming up the hill with her long stride. Ida is very tall, nearly as tall as Alex, and wears a long dark blue woollen coat when it's cold. Since she retired some years ago as the school's Headmistress, she always wears Wellington boots whatever the weather. She tends to wear coloured Wellingtons in the summer, perhaps as a nod to the better weather. She has a unique use for her Wellingtons; she keeps her purse in her right one and folds and stuffs her morning paper in the left one when she has collected it. I watch her stride towards the shop door, try the handle, and then peer in with cupped hands around her eyes. She turned, shaking her head, clearly unhappy that she couldn't pick up her newspaper.

I glanced at Connie who was dozing on the hearth rug, it's hard not to fall asleep on the floor, and particularly on the evil rug. We have "underfloor heating" in this room and, whatever that is, it's great for warming cold paws. Mud from her paws has dried and has fallen into the rug. Anna will be on one of her cleaning missions when she sees it; she's as picky as Mr Featherstone.

Connie was snoring by the time Alex returned from the wholesalers and he didn't look too happy when he climbed out of his large people carrier which he'd backed up to the front of the shop. He wears size thirteen sturdy walking boots. He's very tall, has good shoulders and reddish hair, a bit like Vincent's but Alex is going slightly grey here and there. He has a kind face, laughing blue eyes and loves to talk. Alex unlocked the shop and started unloading boxes of all sizes and colours from the back of the carrier. His trips to and from the shop and his people carrier are interrupted several times by customers which he was happy to serve and chat to.

All the unloading was done and his people carrier was put into the garage by the time Anna reappeared.

I sat up and watched her climb out of her people carrier – a much smaller version to Alex's. Vincent wasn't with her but she'd brought back the towel which was stained a reddish brown with Vincent's blood. Anna's face was sad and blotchy and the knots in my stomach tightened.

I leaped off the sofa and ran along the hall to the doorway leading into the shop and sat by the pet gate. I focused on the shop floor waiting for Anna's moccasins to appear. She likes her moccasins for the shop; these are her third pair; Connie chewed the previous pairs in her puppy stage.

'Where the hell have you been? We won't earn a living if the shop is shut' Alex said gruffly as soon as Anna's moccasins appeared.

'I left you a message on your phone' Anna said.

'I haven't had time to look at my phone, never mind listen to messages' Alex said.

'If you had, you'd have heard my telling you I had to dash Vincent to the Vets' Anna said.

Alex paused, I could see from his face that he'd had chance to take in the towel that Anna held, perhaps even noticed her blotchy face.

'Oh, I see, I'm sorry. What's happened, is he alright? Alex said frowning.

'I found him lying with Claude by the pet door, Connie alerted me. I took one look at him and rang the vets; they admitted him as an emergency.'

'Yes, we know all this, but how is he?' I shouted, which would sound like a long meow. It really is most annoying uprights don't speak feline.

My uprights looked at me and Alex said 'Worried about Vincent?'

'Well yes!' I said, sometimes my uprights can be so slow.

Anna lifted the counter's top and walked towards the pet gate, she bent over it, gave my head a stroke and said the magical words, 'he's going to be okay Claude.' She straightened and turning to Alex said 'He's been in a fight or attacked by some other animal; another cat or a dog, and he'd lost a lot of blood. He needed surgery but with fluids, anti-biotics, and pain relief he should be back with us tomorrow.'

The knots in my tummy undid themselves.

Chapter Four

I was snoozing on the window sill in the dining area of the kitchen. It's a nice spot, particularly if you want to catch the last dregs of the late winter sun before clouds smother it or it sinks away. The sun had long gone when I heard Anna say 'Come through and I'll put the kettle on.'

'Thank you' Esther Dickie said, her voice weary.

Connie's tail wagged and she did her welcome dance; jumping and bouncing gently before spinning around, landing on four paws with her bottom in the air and her tail wagging furiously. Esther sat down at one of the chairs clustered around the dining table and stroked Connie's head, gently tugging her ears in a distracted manner.

I stood, stretched, and jumping down from the window sill wandered over to Esther. I leaped onto the chair next to her to say hello.

'Ah Claude' she said softly and I climbed onto her knee. By the way, I don't just climb on anybody's knee; I'm quite particular. She seems frailer than she did when I left her this morning.

Anna sat down and busied herself pouring out tea from the teapot, very different from the kettle, it doesn't whistle. Esther told Anna the police officers had been very kind. Another officer had turned up who'd covered the window frame with black powder to take finger prints and then helped her get in touch with a local builder for the window to be boarded up.

'The police have given me a crime number but don't hold out much hope of finding the thieves. It's a pity Claude can't talk' Esther said wistfully as she ran her fingers along my back.

'But I can, you just don't speak feline' I meowed.

'Why do you say that?' Anna asked

'Oh, Claude was at the house last night, sitting in the window the thieves left open. I'm sure he'd have seen them' Esther said.

'You are a busy little man' Anna said smiling.

'You didn't tell me' Connie yelped.

'We were looking for Vincent' I said.

'Did you see them?' Connie said.

'Oh yes, size nine trainers, no class to them and size twelve black boots, very dirty but quite well made.'

'And their faces?' Connie said.

'I'd know them if I saw them again' I nodded.

Esther's hand trembled as she stroked my back and I purred, hoping to calm her. Anna also noticed; it was hard not to. Esther's other hand shook as she sipped her tea and rattled the cup in the saucer when she put it down.

'You're welcome to stay here tonight, in fact Esther, I insist you do' Anna said gently.

'That's very kind but, no. I feel I should be at home, although it's different now. Esther's eyes welled with water which trickled down her cheek. 'It isn't the house so much, but you realise it's the things around you that matter, the memories each object has that make it home.'

Anna nodded and said quietly 'What did they take?'

'A frame with a photo of George …. my art deco statue, six crystal swans and my mother's clock; it was an antique when she had it.'

'Not your average thief then, a bit more discerning if they recognised the value of those things' Anna said.

Esther nodded 'I just want my photo back, if nothing else.'

Anna reached over and gave Esther's hand a squeeze.

'I bet they've dumped the photo' Connie said.

I nodded.

'I just wonder how they knew you had such valuable items in your cottage?' Anna said.

Esther blinked at Anna.

I did too, that was a very good point; I've heard that uprights who break into houses usually take televisions and laptops.

'Has anyone been in the house recently that isn't a friend or someone you know well?' Anna said topping up Esther's tea and nudging the milk jug nearer to her.

Esther tipped in a splash of milk and sipped her tea, her forehead crinkled as she thought, and said slowly, 'Yes ... but he was such a nice young man.'

I stopped purring, I needed to hear this clearly.

'Who?' Anna asked.

'I was thinking of the young man that was selling double glazing. I can't think of his name or the company for that matter, but they rang out of the blue, said they were in the area and would I like a quote. As you know, I've wanted to upgrade for a while, so I said yes.'

'When was this?' Anna asked and I meowed the same question.

'It must have been about two weeks ago, although I haven't received the quote yet, but really, I can't see him being part of this, he was utterly charming.'

'Con men usually are' Anna said wryly.

'Any tea left?' Alex said sitting down on another dining chair and reaching for the pot.

Anna looked at him in a distracted way and looked at her watch. 'You should have called me through, I'd have nipped in to help you shut down the shop.'

'It's fine, I've just locked up for now, I'll do it later. Right now, I want to hear everything about this charming young man Esther' Alex said.

'Oh! You think he had something to do with the theft?' Esther said, her eyebrows raising a little.

'It's a possibility' Alex nodded and said 'He would have seen the windows were wooden and old, easy to get into with the right equipment, and seen anything of value, particularly if he's been in every room.'

Anna nodded in agreement.

So did I; that made perfect sense.

'Oh yes, I see what you mean. He did see the whole house to measure the windows.'

'What did he look like? I may know him; he may have been in the shop' Alex said.

'Esther frowned at Alex and Anna, and then shook her head and said 'Well, he was quite slim and smart in a grey suit and spotty tie. He wasn't as tall as you Alex and he had very short brown hair. His face was, well … really …. quite unremarkable and hard to describe.

'Maybe, it would help if you could draw him, or what you remember?' Anna suggested.

'You know, Esther said brightening, that's a good idea, that may help.'

Oh no! It's going to turn into an impromptu art session! I glanced down immediately at Connie who had already started to move; in avoidance mode. She danced next to Alex and pawed at his knee.

'Walk?' Alex said ruffling her ears.

Connie barked 'Yes, let's go now!' Alex gulped down his tea and stood up saying 'I'll leave you ladies to it.'

Alex was quick to get out of the way too, maybe he was in his own avoidance mode?

I jumped from Esther's knee when Anna produced paper, pencils, water colours and pastels which she put down on the table. I walked to Connie whilst Alex put his coat on, and said 'Warnings need to be sent about Retro!'

Connie nodded and said 'Yes, I'm hoping to bump into Duke, but will sound the alarm if I don't', and started dancing around Alex ready to leave.

I made it to the pet door. I've got nothing against art, it's a wonderous thing, when it lands on the canvass or paper and not in my fur. I'm named after one of Anna's favourite artists, Claude Monet, a

French Impressionist. I like my name and Vincent likes his too. He's been called after another of Anna's heroes, Vincent Van Gough. I remember the long debate Anna and Alex had about Connie's name. After throwing around a lot of names between them, which didn't seem to fit a golden ball of fur with long floppy ears and pudgy legs (she did have pudgy legs when she was a pup), Alex said he'd always admired the painter, John Constable. Anna agreed she rather liked his work but, they also agreed, that standing in the middle of a field yelling "Constable" or asking "Constable" to "sit" in the street may lead to awkward situations, particularly if a police officer was nearby. With this in mind, and as she was a girl, they shortened Constable to Connie, and I think it suits her.

My whiskers twitched at the sight of the brushes being unleashed but relaxed a little, it was water colour, they washed out easily enough, but it still meant water was involved. I headed out, retreating through the pet door and into the evening air.

I'd not realised it had been raining again and there was a washed twang in the air.

'Hello Uncle Claude, is Vincent coming out soon?' a soft young voice from the top of the fence to my left said.

'Hello Mabel' I said and walked to the fence and leaped up to join her.

Mabel is a pale smoky grey cat with white tips on her ears and front paws. She's about the same age as Vincent. She's not a British

Shorthaired, like Vincent and I, but a Ragdoll. Her fur is longer and she grooms it a lot. She has a bit of a squashed muzzle which is typical of her kind. Ragdoll's famously go limp when picked up, and Mabel has that down to a fine art.

'I've been waiting for ages' Mabel said a little petulantly.

'I'm afraid he won't be out tonight' I said.

'Is he being kept indoors?'

'In a manner of speaking, yes. Why were you kept indoors last night? I asked.

'Oh, my people didn't like the gift I gave them' she shrugged.

'What type; dead or alive?'

'Very much alive. I thought I'd give Sue and Theo a change as mice don't seem to go down too well.'

'What was it?' I asked intrigued.

'I brought them a frog, but I'm never touching another one again; horrible tasting slimy thing it was. Anyway, I dropped it when I got indoors and it jumped into my water pot. That was a bit annoying as I wanted a drink but it just sat there, and I watched it for ages.'

'What happened?'

'Sue must have thought I needed my pot refilling. She was half asleep and when she picked the water pot up, and the frog jumped out. She shrieked; you know what Sue's like.'

'Yes, we do call her Shrieking Sue' I said.

'Exactly, well she dropped the pot. There was water everywhere. Theo rushed in to see what was going on. It was kind of funny, my uprights on their hands and knees chasing a frog. They eventually cornered it by the bin, pushed it into a plastic box and took it outside. The stupid thing just sat there on the patio in their box and they locked me in, perhaps thinking I'd bring it in again.'

I nodded; it really is a mystery why uprights don't like our gifts. Perhaps if we wrapped them with pretty paper, tied with bows, it may be different?

'So why can't Vincent come out? Mabel asked as she licked her paw and washed behind her ear.

'He's not actually here at the moment' I said.

Mabel stopped preening her ear and peered at me.

'He's at the Vets' I said gently.

Mabel gulped, her eyes widening and said 'Is he going to …. come home?'

'Yes of course, but he may not be out and about for a bit.'

'What happened?' Mabel asked.

'Retro.'

Mabel's eyes widened and she said 'No!' and started looking around, agitated, with her ears tweaked forward.

'Yes, I'll need to confirm of course, but I don't think Vincent would have said Retro unless it was' I said.

'What are you going to do?

'I'm off to see Monty. It may lead to a Council meeting but in the meantime, we need to warn the community. Connie is out with Alex and she's hoping to meet Duke. The canines have a right to know, after all, he attacked Tyson, that little Pekinese chap who now has a permanent squint. There may even be a Canine Chorus to get the news around the village so don't be alarmed.

'Tyson - that was Retro?' Mabel whispered, shocked.

I nodded 'Yes, very messy it was. The canines got jumpy about that and it has taken a while for relations to recover. The canines will know, as well as we do, Retro shouldn't be back.'

Mabel nodded 'Can I help?'

'We need to alert the felines. Caterwauling isn't going to work, he'll hear; so, can you start a warning whisper advising all felines need to be in pairs when possible, and youngsters such as yourself, to be indoors after 8 pm, until Retro is dealt with.'

Mabel nodded and said 'I'll go and see Roly now, and start a whisper.'

'Good, thank you, but make sure you are in by 8 pm, the curfew applies to you too.'

Mabel nodded and said forlornly 'Will do, it's not much fun without Vincent anyway.'

I nodded 'I'm off to see Monty, and warn the squirrels.'

Chapter Five

Quiff is an old friend of mine. He's a squirrel, but I don't hold that against him, and neither do the rest of the feline community. He's an honorary member of the Council, sitting on behalf of and a voice for the village squirrels. We all believe that thumbless beings should stick together, whether living with uprights or not, and especially in times of danger.

All the squirrel community are wild. There are various scurries living in Dale Wood, about three miles from here, but some squirrels, like Quiff, live in the village trees. Quiff's drey, made from sticks, twigs and dried leaves is very cosy, lodged high in the branches of the tall, large, lime tree which staddles the boundary at the bottom of Sebastian Draycott's and Nick and Aresha Desai's gardens. Monty's uprights are the Desais.

Quiff isn't someone who likes to be out and about late at night and prefers to get up early in the mornings. He's usually busy when the birds start their chatter at dawn. I'm more of a night-time being and like to watch dawn appear. If I've not had an eventful night, I like to be around the pet gate to the shop early in the mornings, shoe spot and listen to the children's chatter after breakfast. I missed shoe-spotting and the children this morning but there's always tomorrow.

The quickest way to Quiff and Monty's is by walking to the bottom of our garden, walking down the length of Mr Featherstone's side fence, which stretches by his house, and jump down onto the driveway at the front.

I must admit; I enjoy the grid pattern of the fences, it's a very helpful way of getting around. However, I'm not a fan of the road, a grey ribbon of tarmac that goes sticky in summer when it's hot or covered in ice in winter when it's very cold, neither of which is good for paws. The road sits between the front of Mr Featherstone's house which I need to cross to get to the front of Quiff and Monty's homes.

People carriers whiz up and down the road most of the day. When it's dark, the carriers put on their twin lights which glare, blinding most of us thumbless beings. It really is a flaw of uprights, not having night vision and needing to put lights in carriers.

The road is quiet and I made my way across to Sebastian Draycott's home. He has a patch of lawn in his front garden and a driveway to the side of the house. His own people carrier is parked in the driveway but there is room to squeeze by it. He's a bit fussy about his carrier which he polishes a lot. He's also a bit short sighted, both physically and in his attitude, but he's not a Nasty, like Trainers and Boots.

Nasties are people and occasionally, although it's rare, felines like Retro. I've not come across a canine Nasty yet. Thankfully, there aren't many Nasties around but I know when I've met one. When I was younger, I had mistaken some uprights who'd been gruff and hard to get on with as Nasties. I leant that life had given them knocks and disappointment and they may have been unhappy but they weren't Nasties. Nasties are selfish and, well nasty individuals who put themselves first and suck away others happiness and well-being.

I've walked the length of Mr Draycott's people carrier a couple of times, leaving a trail of paw prints from the boot, over the roof and along the bonnet. The paw prints aren't particularly large or caked in mud but do leave a distinct impression. I thought I was carrying on the principles of my namesake, Claude Monet, whose art work is fuzzy, with few defined lines, contrasting light and dark, but Mr Draycott didn't see it like that. I've not walked over the car since Monty was blamed for the last set of paw-prints I did.

Monty lives next door, and Mr Draycott complained to his people, Nick and Aresha Desai. Monty told me Aresha was rather good. She listened patiently to Mr Draycott's complaint about the paw prints on his car. She asked to see the evidence, and told him with arms folded, that Monty couldn't possibly have been responsible for the paw-prints, as they were made by a four-legged cat, Monty has three legs.

It's true, Monty left one of his legs at the Vets; they lost it somewhere in their surgery. Nick Desai took him there when he'd been knocked down by a large and wide people carrier that was going too fast.

Monty didn't seem to mind that he'd only got three legs at first, but then got very down when he realised he couldn't jump as high as he once did. He took to staying in his garden a lot more. Quiff, his scurry and us felines rallied around him and still visit him often. His uprights don't seem to mind others visiting, which is a good thing, as Monty is an Elder of the Council.

I jumped onto the fence between Mr Draycott and the Desai's gardens. Monty wasn't in his garden, so I walked down the fence line to the lime tree at the bottom. I looked up. It's quite a climb to get to Quiff's drey, so I shouted 'Hello!'

'Err hello' Quiff responded from somewhere on the ground to my right. He sounded distracted and I couldn't see him.

'Where are you?'

'I'm here' Quiff said as he backed out from under a conifer shrub, his large bushy tail appearing first.

I jumped off the fence and ambled over to him. He wasn't paying much attention to me but scrabbling at the ground, muttering to himself, and peering amongst the ivy creeping along the ground.

I sat down and curled my tail around my feet, which, by the way, is the polite way to sit. I watched him for a moment or two, and said 'Have you lost something?'

Quiff stood up on his back legs, his thick bushy tail twitching behind him and sighed, a heavy ladened sigh; one of those when you are explaining something obvious and which should be obvious to everyone else without having to explain. 'Yes, Nuts!'

'Oh, and they should be here?'

'What! Well of course they should be here, what's the point in looking for them here if I'd put them somewhere else?' Quiff said in exasperation.

I shrugged 'Just checking.'

Quiff stared at me, sneezed, and shook his head impatiently. He hopped to the left and started scrabbling at the creeping ivy again.

I heard the Desai's pet door clatter and saw Monty saunter towards me with a gait that was his own. Monty is black like me but, unlike me, he has a white chest which makes him look like Alex when he has his dinner jacket on; very smart and debonair.

'Hello Claude, good to see you.' Monty said sitting down next to me and after looking at Quiff continued 'Has he lost his nuts again?'

'Yes ... What do you mean again?' I said.

'He's getting very forgetful. I had to aim him at his drey last Thursday, he'd forgotten where he'd built it.'

'Hmm, why doesn't he use his nose?' I asked.

'He has a snuffle; noses are not much use with a snuffle' Monty said.

I watched Quiff scurry to another part of the garden. He looked like he was dancing, moving up, down and side to side with his head bobbing. He suddenly stopped and shouted 'Aha! there you are! ... oooh you're not a nut' and threw the object over his shoulder which landed near me.

I looked at it – a pebble.

I looked at Monty who shook his head.

'Aha!' Quiff said again loudly.

'That doesn't look like a nut' I said to Monty.

'It isn't; it's a daffodil bulb. My uprights planted a group of them last year, I don't know how many he's dug up now, but the flowers they are expecting are not going to appear' Monty said.

I nodded.

'It may take a while, but he'll find them, so what can I do for you Claude, or is this a social call? Monty said.

'It's always good to see you, but I'm here to report a Section 2 breach of the Cat Code'

Monty's green eyes glinted and he said 'A serious breach. Who's the perpetrator?'

'It appears to have been Retro' I said.

Monty was silent for a moment and we watched Quiff.

'Who was the victim?' Monty said quietly.

'Vincent.'

Monty shot a quick look at me and said in a voice that was slightly husky 'How is he?'

I sighed said 'He's at the Vets, but my uprights say he should be back tomorrow.'

Monty shuddered at the word Vets. He nodded and said after a while 'Vincent is too young to have met Retro; how confident is he it was him?'

'Vincent was in no fit state to answer questions but he was pretty sure it was. When he gets home, I'll find out more' I said.

'If it is indeed Retro, he won't be alone' Monty said.

'Yes, I'd be surprised if his crew aren't nearby; he's too much of a coward to be around here on his own.'

Monty nodded and said 'We'll need to warn all the feline, canine and squirrel communities and I'll call a meeting for tomorrow night.'

'Mabel and Roly are starting a warning whisper. Connie is out with Alex and hopes to meet Duke. Whether Connie alerts him or not, let's hope Retro doesn't speak canine; there may be a Canine Chorus but that's out of our control.'

Monty nodded.

Another daffodil bulb rolled towards us and stopped inches from my feet.

'Aha!! There you are!' startling both of us; Quiff can make a lot of noise for a little chap.

Quiff jumped towards us with a huge nut in his hands. 'Found it just where I put it' he said nodding vigorously.

'Mmm .. Are the others that you've stored with that one? I said.

'Of course' Quiff nodded, puffing out his chest.

'It may be a good idea to use a marker, a heap of pebbles perhaps, so you don't forget where you found that one' I said.

'Are you suggesting that I've lost my marbles?' Quiff said huffily.

'No, just the nuts' I said.

Quiff pushed his nut under one arm, sniffed and ignoring me said to Monty 'What have you two been talking about, you look very serious?'

'It appears Retro has attacked young Vincent' Monty said.

'Oh no, he's back, what's he doing here!' Quiff took a step backwards, his eyes darting around him.

'I don't know. Can you warn the other squirrels, and keep an eye out for him from your dreys and, if you spot him, let me know. We'll hold a Council meeting tomorrow night' Monty said.

Quiff nodded vigorously.

'There's one more thing Quiff, it's just occurred to me that you could help with the view you have from your drey' I said.

'Yes?' Quiff hopped forward.

'Did you spot two uprights, males, one short and skinny, the other taller, both wearing black and leaving Esther Dickie's cottage last night?' I asked.

Quiff rubbed his ears with his free hand and said 'I can't see Esther's cottage from my drey but …. I did wake up in the middle of the night and saw two males leaving Mr Featherstone's driveway. They were in a hurry. One was carrying something wrapped in a cloth and the other was carrying a bag. I could do with a bag like that' Quiff said wistfully.

'And .. where did they go?' I said.

'Ohh, … they got into a people carrier with no windows and they ran it down the hill before turning the lights on. When they got to the bottom of the hill, the engine fired up and they drove off.'

'Which way did they go?' I said.

'They turned left on Amble Road' towards the estate' Quiff said.

'If the people carrier had no windows, did it have any signs on it? You know how uprights like to paint their carriers' I asked.

Quiff's eyes sparkled and he hugged his nut. He grinned, his two large teeth shining white and said 'Oh yes, it had an enormous acorn painted on the side; a beautiful thing it was.'

'Why are you so interested in these uprights Claude?' Monty asked.

'They stole things from Esther's cottage last night. The things are important to Esther and she wants them back' I said.

Monty nodded his eyes gleaming and said 'Esther's a Kinder, so anything the Council can do to help, let me know.'

'Thank you; can you authorise extra patrols around Esther's home and an official caterwaul? I need to know where the people carrier is with the acorn on the side.'

Monty nodded and said 'We'll do it tonight.'

Chapter Six

Although it's only mid-morning, Connie is flat out on her back with her paws in the air, snoring. To be fair, Anna had taken her out at dawn for a long run across the fields that separate the village from the next town. If she wasn't particularly tired when she got back, she's got next to no chance of staying awake with the combination of a hearty breakfast, the underfloor heating that seeps through the evil rug and the glow of the embers from the wood burner.

I'm on the back of the sofa by the front window, in my sphinx pose, waiting for Anna to arrive in her people carrier with Vincent. I'm feeling a little tired too but I can't sleep; I want to see Vincent.

I've been out most of the night. Having left Monty and Quiff, I followed Alex who walked Esther home after she had finished her painting of the double-glazing sales-man who I'm calling Spotty Tie Man. I'd watched Alex check the boarded-up kitchen window was secure. He'd gone into Esther's home and I'd seen him at the rear windows on the first floor, checking that they were all tightly closed.

I'd swung by Esther's home throughout the night, and prowling around the garden I met Jasper. Jasper is a Maine Coon who is hard to miss, with his white body splattered with black patches and large ears. He is a very big cat and the sort of friend you want with you in a crisis. He doesn't say a great deal but he isn't shy. He told me once he didn't see the point in talking for the sake of filling in silence, unless it was worth the bother of saying something useful. Jasper's uprights are the McKenzies, an elderly couple, who are friends with Esther. Jasper reported that he hadn't seen as much as a mouse around Esther's home on his Patrol, before he nodded goodbye and strolled off to continue his Patrol on other Kinders' homes.

I watch the usual customers come and go and I nod to the occasional canine I recognise. Most canines are tied to the front sign post, perhaps because their uprights think they'll wander off ? I'm not sure why dogs are tied up in such a manner, but most don't seem to mind and sit patiently chatting to each other. Duke the Doberman, the leader of the local canine community has turned up with his upright, a clean faced youngish man who wears size eleven, good quality trainers with a green tick along the sides and thick black soles; quite stylish if you like that sort of thing. Duke is tall, with long powerful legs and shoulders. He's black apart from his eyebrows which are smudges of brown. I've never seen Duke wearing a lead, he's far too polite and well-mannered to need such a thing and his upright respects that. I also have a lot of respect for Duke, and nod at him through the window. He nods back, and does it quite regally, well anyone of his stature nodding would appear stately. Duke was responsible for calming the canines down when Retro beat up Tyson four months ago and Connie told me she'd bumped into him on her walk yesterday evening.

At last, Anna's people carrier arrives and I watch as she parks it in front of the garage, leaving plenty of room for other people carriers to pull up and use the shop.

'They're here!' I said.

Connie stirred and stretched as I leaped from the back of the sofa onto the floor and walked into the hall.

A gust of cold air invaded the warmth as the front door opened to announce the arrival of Anna with Vincent in the cat carrier.

The cat carrier is universal and used by both Vincent and I on the rare occasions we have to go to the Vets. I am not a fan of the cat carrier. Unlike a people carrier, it has no wheels, pedals or engine. It's a plastic box with slattered holes either side, mesh doors at both ends and a handle on the top. I've had a lot of fun (Anna and Alex call it a fight) to get me into the cat carrier. They always work in pairs, a bit like good cop, bad cop on the TV. One of them thinks they are distracting me with a juicy piece of fish cake whilst the other, usually wearing oven gloves, sneaks up behind to grab and bundle me inside the waiting carrier. Anna and Alex can be very determined and, I must admit, they tend to win. I'd got my own back at the Vets, when I'd refused to come out. That tactic did work well, until one determined Vet dismantled the cat carrier by taking the top off. Imagine my shock. It was a while before I got over that, and I ignored Anna for a few days, turning my back on her when she came anywhere near me.

Anna placed the cat carrier on the floor and started her boot boogie; hopping around on one foot whilst trying to get her grey, mid-heeled leather boot off the other. Connie sat in the open doorway of the sitting room with a fascinated look on her face whilst she watched Anna's boogying. I usually enjoy the spectacle too, but not today.

Whilst Anna is distracted with her boots I circle the cat carrier, and peer in through the slats. I can smell the disinfectant, which is worse than the turps Anna uses to clean her art brushes.

'What are you doing?' Connie said.

'I'm checking' I said.

'Checking what' Connie said, standing up.

'That he has all his legs' I said.

'Why wouldn't he have all his legs? Connie said walking towards the cat carrier.

'He should, but you never know, after what happened to Monty; its best to be sure.'

'And does he?' Connie asked.

'Yes, all four legs are attached and present, but the Vets have taken away large areas of his fur, and he's wearing a cone strapped around his collar.'

Connie shuddered, a look of disgust crossing her face and said 'Not the cone!'

I nodded and said 'That will come off soon enough. Let's hope Vincent deals with his cone better than you did.'

'Don't remind me, seven whole days of misery' Connie said, shaking her head.

'Vincent's is smaller than yours, how much damage can he do?'

'Hmmm, his head is nearer to the floor than mine was' she pondered, peering in through the slats of the cat carrier.

'At least Alex and Anna's shins shouldn't be too battered but our legs will probably take the brunt' I said.

Anna had finally slipped her indoor moccasins on, and hanging her coat up with the others, she gently picked up the cat carrier and we followed her into the kitchen/diner.

I'm surprised she didn't take Vincent into the sitting room, but then again, Anna is aware (aren't we all) of Vincent's deep hatred of the rug. She placed the cat carrier by the radiator in the dining part of the room, got onto her knees and said, 'Now Vincent, we'll put you here where it's warm to sleep it off.' She dismantled the top of the cat carrier, and took off the doors. She stroked his head gently, but he didn't move.

She glanced at Connie and I, and smiling said 'Don't worry you two, he's a bit groggy from the anaesthetic, but will be right as rain soon.'

Alex popped into the kitchen and said 'Is he okay?'

'Anna nodded, and said 'He will be; we have antibiotics for him.'

'Okay, I'll fire up the oven gloves, we're going to need them if he's anything like Claude taking his medicine, hey Claude?' Alex said, raising his eyebrows.

Well really! How am I to know whether something is good for me or not? My uprights may not speak feline, but I understand their language well enough. If they just explained what they were giving me, I may be more inclined to co-operate. Having said that, I'm not convinced anything from the Vets is good for me.

'Hello! A voice was heard from the shop and Alex disappeared.

'Okay guys, you look after Vincent and I'll be back soon' Anna said, as she stood and headed for the shop to help Alex, leaving us staring at Vincent.

'Has she gone yet?' Vincent whispered, his mouth barely moving.

I looked at him, his eyes were still closed and he hadn't moved a muscle.

'Erm, yes' Connie said.

Vincent opened his eyes a little and said 'You sure?'

'The room is completely empty of uprights' I said.

Vincent let out a sigh of relief 'Good! I like Anna but she keeps crying when she looks at me and I can't bear it. She's worse than Shrieking Sue when she's like this.'

'She's been worried about you, Alex has too, we all have' Connie said.

'Hmm, I get that, but Anna's turned into a watering can' Vincent said.

'People's eyes leak when they are sad or happy; she can't help it' I said.

'Well I'm alright now, so hopefully her eyes will stop leaking and … maybe what would help, is if you can get this thing off my head.'

'The cone has to stay on' Connie said matter of factly.

'Why?'

'It's a rite of passage to wear it, when released from the Vets' I said.

Connie nodded 'That's right, I had mine on for a week.'

'But, I have an itch and I can't get at it' Vincent wailed.

'That's the point of a cone' Connie said gently.

Vincent started shaking his head, and the cone wobbled around. 'Hmph, but I can't get through the pet door with this thing on.'

'That's the other point, you won't be going outside until it comes off' I said.

'What!! I have to be ... indoors ... all the time ... and use the cat litter tray!' Vincent wailed.

Connie nodded and said 'Get used to it, time will soon pass.'

I nodded and said 'Yes, and by the time you're free of the cone, Retro will have been dealt with.'

'I want to put Retro in a cone' Vincent said flicking his tail in annoyance.

'You're not big enough yet' I said.

Vincent jutted his chin forward which made the cone go upwards, I tried not to laugh and said 'There's no need to have a strop, but tell me, how did you know it was Retro?'

Vincent blinked at me and said 'Because the tatty old tabby that was with him said "that's enough Retro, leave him", when he'd pinned me down and was about to strike again.'

I felt a chill run through my whiskers and down my tail. I glanced at Connie who looked uncomfortable.

Vincent slumped, sighed deeply, and said, 'I've survived death by Retro to end dying of boredom wearing a cone.'

I put the news Vincent had given to the back of my mind, and said in a voice that I hoped sounded positive, 'Well, that's where you're wrong, you can be involved in an …. important mission, a bit like a pre-training exercise before you join the Cadets' I said.

Connie looked at me bewildered but Vincent's ears pricked forward, his big eyes blinking at me.

'What mission?' Vincent said eagerly.

'You can be a look out' I said.

'Look out what?' Vincent's little forehead furrowed.

'Uprights' I said.

'Uprights?' Vincent said looking disgusted, 'That doesn't sound like much of a mission, I can look at uprights every day.'

'Yes, but we need to be on the look-out for three males, one wearing size nine trainers, small and skinny and has the look of a rat about him, the other wears size twelve black boots and is taller and much heavier, the third wears a spotty tie with very short hair. We can show you a sketch of Spotty Tie Man which Esther did. They should be driving a windowless people carrier with a large acorn painted on the side.'

Vincent nodded and then asked 'Why do we need to find them?'

Connie explained what had happened to Esther. Vincent was shocked, and after reassuring him that Esther was shaken and sad, but okay physically, he wanted to help, and put them in a cone too.

To carry out his mission, I thought it was best to get him onto the top of the settee in the sitting room, so he could look out from the front window. Connie and I debated the best way to do this, and by the time we'd come up with a plan which, unfortunately, would involve Vincent punching his claws in the fabric of the settee (sometimes it can't be helped), Vincent had dozed off.

Chapter Seven

Connie and I have been busy, in and out of the pet door all morning, to see Vincent's well-wishers.

The first to arrive were Peanut and Pickle. They are both Domestic Shorthairs, although I think Peanut's ancestry has links to the Siamese line. She's quite tall with long legs and is the colour of well, a peanut, except for her chocolate-coloured ears and tail. I like Peanut, she's a very sensible sort and takes everything in her long-legged stride. Pickle's coat is the colour of rich brown chutney. Both live with an upright called Mrs Duncan who has the habit of naming her felines with food items.

Pickle is very interested in climbing anything that can be clambered up, and is Vincent's idol. In her kittenhood days, I'd heard on the cat-chat that she'd got herself into trouble with Mrs Duncan for climbing up a thick brocade curtain which hung against the sitting room window. She was found hanging from it. She'd been unable to retract a claw and Mrs Duncan had to climb on a chair to untangle her from the material. I don't think she's made another attempt at curtain climbing, but I wouldn't put it past her to try again.

Peanut and Pickle are both a little older than Vincent and Mabel. They have turned one, in upright years, and are in March's Cat Cadets; a group Monty now trains on behalf of March, our Grand Elder. He teaches the Cadets the Cat Code, which is the law felines abide by.

Monty also sorts out their training schedules and organises Patrols of the Kinders, which the Cadets also get involved with.

Kinders are uprights who don't have their own thumbless companions to live with, but who are kind to us. We keep an eye on our Kinders, checking in with them to see if they are alright. We do this in sequence, after all, it would be bad if all felines visited a Kinder on the same day or night and then no one looked in on them for a week. Kinders often give us a drink or food, which isn't asked for, but always well received.

I have to say seeing Peanut and Pickle along with Roly, who'd somehow managed to heft his very solid, almost round, tortoiseshell body over the fence to enquire after Vincent was the better part of the morning.

Vincent isn't an easy invalid, in fact, he isn't very polite when he's wearing a cone. He seems to have forgotten how to be himself. Since he woke up from his snooze, he tried to cajole Connie and I into believing that he would be far more effective at looking for Trainers, Boots and Spotty Tie Man without the cone. He didn't get very far, and became adamant that if we wouldn't help him, he'd get rid of the cone himself.

Connie thinks he's possibly the worst being, thumbless or otherwise, she's ever known at being a patient. I reminded her that patience wasn't one of his strong points at the best of times. This fact seemed to irritate her even more and she accused me of stating the obvious.

I'd been trying to reason with him, during his last attempt at trying to dislodge the cone from his head. This time, he'd backed himself in between two of the dining chairs, with his body on one side of the chair legs, and his cone on the other. He twisted his head one way, then the other, and started tugging at the cone trapped between the chair legs. He tugged so hard that the chairs parted and Vincent hurtled backwards, knocking Mabel off her legs who had just walked in.

Mabel has an open invitation to our home. She's the only other feline allowed in as Anna and Alex are friends with Shrieking Sue and Theo.

Mabel wasn't happy about being knocked over, but Vincent was pleased to see her. This was short lived when she also refused to help him remove the cone. Unlike us, she yelled at him to stop being such a fuss-puss and then pinned him down and gave him a wash. I waited for the inevitable fight, but to my and Connie's utter astonishment, he gave way and allowed her to preen him.

Connie escaped, with her ears flouncing and tail quite still and headed for the evil rug in the sitting room, muttering darkly about Retro and the Vets having a lot to answer for, and, by all that was canine, they would pay at some indistinct point in the future.

I followed her and watched her slump down with a grateful sigh. I decided not to say anything. I didn't want to be accused of stating the obvious again but I know that getting the Vets to answer for anything is a big ask. The best she could do would be to pee on them when she goes to the Vets again, but she wouldn't like to do that, she's too well mannered. Retro remained high on my "to do list", not just for attacking Vincent but inflicting an ill-tempered Vincent on us.

I've left Connie snoozing on the evil rug. Whilst Mabel is keeping Vincent quiet, I'm restoring my sanity by lying in semi-sphinx pose (front paws curled in), at my preferred place by the pet gate, for a bit of shoe spotting. I know if I lie down, I'd do a Connie and probably doze off.

Both Alex and Anna are in the shop. Maybe they knew Vincent was going to be a handful and it is their way of escaping? Alex is behind the counter, on the computer, printing off reams of bills to attach to the Saturday morning papers tomorrow, when they are delivered to uprights homes by the paper boys and girls. Anna is cleaning and re-stocking shelves in a rhythmic, methodical manner and her moccasins pass by the pet gate, to venture into the stock room at the back of the shop and out again, with boxes of goods to display.

A pair of sensible highly polished boots below long black trousers appear in my line of vision. The face that appears above the counter is a middle-aged man. He has salt and pepper hair and the sort of face that has been grown into, with lines across his forehead and deep laughter lines fanning out around his eyes. He has very large bushy eyebrows and a ruddy nose which has been outdoors more than inside. He is wearing a police uniform with highly polished silver buttons, stripes on his sleeves and his hat is underneath his arm.

'Hi, how can I help Officer?' Alex says with a smile.

'Hello, I'm Sergeant Wisby' he said as he held out an ID card in front of him. 'I'm carrying out door to door enquiries following an incident that took place at 38 Tottle Hill on Wednesday night.'

'Oh, the break in at Esther Dickie's house?' Alex said.

Sergeant Wisby nodded and said, 'That's right, can you tell me whether you saw anything suspicious during the evening of the 24th?'

I sat up. 'I saw them', I meowed loudly.

Sergeant Wisby looked at me and smiled, the lines around his eyes fanning out. I thought for one moment he understood feline but, no.

'We didn't see or hear anything I'm afraid' Alex said.

'But we have our own theory' Anna said walking up to the counter.

'Oh, and what would that be', Sergeant Wisby said, his eyebrows rising.

'Well, it seemed to us that the items that were taken were not your run of the mill items that most thieves take.'

Sergeant Wisby nodded.

'We asked Esther if there had been anyone at the house recently that she didn't really know. She told us a representative from a double-glazing company had called about two weeks ago. He'd measured all the windows, and would have seen anything of value in Esther's cottage.'

Sergeant Wisby's eyebrows rose higher.

I wish I had eyebrows like his, they are impressive and seemed to have a life of their own.

'That's interesting, I'll have a chat with Mrs Dickie about that' Sergeant Wisby said.

'Yes, okay, but she couldn't remember his name, or the company for that matter. She couldn't really describe him either, but she was upset of course' Anna said.

'That's understandable' Sergeant Wisby said.

'But Anna had the bright idea of asking Esther to draw him. I'll go and fetch the drawing if that would help?' Alex said.

'Yes please' Sergeant Wisby said, nodding.

I quickly moved out of the way whilst Alex dashed through the pet gate and returned with the drawing. I sat again and watched Alex hand the picture to Sergeant Wisby saying, 'We don't recognise him.'

Sergeant Wisby looked at it and said 'He has a very spotty tie. It's a pity that's the most remarkable thing about him.'

He took out his phone from his top pocket and photographed the picture, checking that he had the image, before putting his phone away. He handed the picture back to Alex and looked around the shop. Unlike most people he didn't look at the shelves but at the ceiling.

'Do you have CCTV in here?' Sergeant Wisby said.

'Yes, a camera is trained just about where you are standing, one on the door and another is just outside' Alex said.

Sergeant Wisby nodded and said 'How long do you keep the footage for?'

'It re-records on a rolling seven-day basis' Alex said.

'Can I have a look at the footage for the 24th, the thieves may have used a vehicle which may be caught on your exterior camera' Sergeant Wisby said.

'No it won't, they used a people carrier parked outside Monty and Quiff's upright's houses' I said.

'Chatty, isn't he, that cat of yours' Sergeant Wisby said nodding towards me.

'Yes, Esther thinks he saw the thieves; it's almost as if he is trying to tell us something' Anna said.

'I am, and one day, one of you will speak feline!

'I'll get the footage for the 24th. You'll need to come around here to view the screen' Alex said, hitting buttons on the computer. Sergeant Wisby, followed by Anna, passed by the gate and they all focused on the computer screen.

'What's going on?' Connie said yawning as she walked towards me and sat down, her tail swishing the floor.

'It's a police officer, Sergeant Wisby, he's asking questions about the theft at Esther's.'

'He has impressive eyebrows' Connie said, looking at Sergeant Wisby's profile.

I nodded and said, 'Wait until you see his whole face, they are more dramatic head on.'

Sergeant Wisby turned and looked at us, his eyebrows raising and said 'Who do we have here then?'

'That's Connie' Anna said glancing down at us.

'I see what you mean, I want a pair of eyebrows like that, so expressive' Connie sighed.

'Me too' I said.

'They seem to be very good friends' Sergeant Wisby said.

'Oh yes, they are; they get on like a house on fire' Anna said, glancing at us and smiling before she turned to look at the computer screen.

'Is that a good thing?' Connie asked uncertainly.

'What?' I said.

'A house on fire.'

She has a point.

'It's great to see a dog and cat get along. I only wish we could learn from their example, after all we are all people' Sergeant Wisby said wistfully.

'He seems to think it's a good thing to get on like a house on fire' I said.

Connie flopped down and did her own sphinx pose and said 'Hmm, maybe it's one of the expressions uprights have, you know, like the one Anna came out with this morning, when she said Vincent would be as right as rain.'

'That's an even more stupid expression than getting on like a house on fire; what can possibly be right about rain' I said, shuddering at the thought of getting wet.

'Here we are, I've started the footage from 7 pm on Wednesday evening, and I'll fast forward but pause if we see anything' Alex said.

Sergeant Wisby nodded and they all peered at the screen.

'I didn't know they had a TV in there' Connie said, sounding surprised.

'It's not a regular TV' I said.

'It doesn't seem to matter, look, they're all in that trance like state as if it is' Connie said.

'You know what uprights are like with TV's, although I do quite like watching the programmes that show different places' I said.

'Vincent's quite fond of watching snooker too' Connie said.

'Well, there are balls involved, so nothing new there' I said.

Anna sighed and said 'Oh dear, there doesn't appear to be anything on the tape that will help.'

'No, but worth having a look. I'll get off now, but thank you for your assistance' Sergeant Wisby said.

Sergeant Wisby walked to the gate and winked at me as he passed by.

'Why did he wink at you?' Connie muttered.

'No idea, maybe it's his way of saying goodbye.'

Chapter Eight

Alex took Connie for a walk after Sergeant Wisby left and Anna manned the shop. The prospect of entertaining Vincent wasn't appealing to Connie, and she told me she hoped Alex was prepared for a very long walk.

I ambled back into the kitchen to see what Vincent and Mabel were up to, and found them both asleep. I quietly made my escape through the pet door which turned out to be good timing as Peanut appeared on top of the fence at the bottom of the garden.

'Claude, come quickly!' Peanut shouted.

I raced towards her 'What is it, has Retro been found?' I said.

Peanut shook her head and said 'No but Quiff has spotted the people carrier with the Acorn painted on it. Monty is organising a Pursuit.'

I leaped onto the fence and followed her quickly along the fence-line of Mr Featherstone's garden and jumping off, ran down his drive and over the ribbon of tarmac. We ran down the garden of the Desais and bumped into Quiff who was hopping excitedly from one foot to the other. Monty sat waiting and stood when he saw Pickle and I dash towards him.

'Well done Pickle. Hello Claude, everything's ready, I just want you to identify that we have the right people carrier and I'll authorise a Pursuit' Monty said.

'Claude, follow me!' Quiff said and leaped up the lime tree.

I don't mind a spot of tree climbing, but I'm not a squirrel. We felines climb, Squirrels scurry and leap from one branch to another.

I clambered up the lime tree. The bark isn't particularly smooth so it's quite easy to get a grip. I may not be as nimble as Quiff, who scoffed that I was slow, but within a couple of minutes I joined him on a branch about half way up the tree.

Quiff was bouncing on the branch as he gazed at the people carrier which was parked two streets away on Victoria Avenue. I thought it was outside number 42, but I couldn't see the door with the number on it, as it was obscured by the roof of the bungalow in front of me.

'Ahhh, just look at the size of that acorn, isn't it wonderful' Quiff said quivering.

I shook my head and sighed, I don't want to dampen the little chap's enthusiasm, after all, it is a pretty good painting of an acorn. Anna says that art should bring out an emotional response. I can honestly say, paintings of an oversized acorn brings out an emotional response in Quiff.

'I'm glad you like the acorn, but it's the uprights using that people carrier that I want to see' I said.

'Oh yes, of course, but even you have to admit that the acorn is a thing of beauty' Quiff said wistfully.

Just to shut him up, although Connie would accuse me of being patronizing, I said 'Yes of course it is.'

I settled down on the branch to wait for movement around the people carrier. Quiff continued to sigh contentedly next to me as he gazed at the acorn, but at least he was quiet.

After about the twentieth sigh from Quiff, a thin young man with a rat like face appeared down the path from the house and headed for the passenger door of the people carrier. He was wearing blue overalls but I couldn't see his shoes from my viewpoint. It was Trainers though; I'd recognise him anywhere. He was followed closely by two others, the first one, stocky and broad, I recognised him as Boots. The third was tall and slim and I assumed he was Spotty Tie Man although he wasn't wearing a tie but had overalls on.

I stood and looked down at Monty who was sat on the ground. 'Yes, these are the uprights I'm looking for' I shouted.

Monty nodded and turned to Peanut and said 'Start the Pursuit.'

I watched Peanut jump gracefully onto the fence at the back of the Desai's garden and sprint along the lawned garden until she disappeared by the front of the bungalow. I heard her caterwauling the message to other waiting felines. I suspected Pickle and Roly would be involved along with the other Cadets.

Pursuits end in success or failure. Successful Pursuits happen when the uprights being pursued live in our district. I only hope these Nasties live nearby. Time will tell, and all I can do now is wait, although I won't be waiting here sat in the tree, which is quite draughty without any leaves. Quiff has stopped sighing and I glance at him; he looks quite thoughtful.

'Thank you for your help' I said.

Quiff nodded.

'Are you going up to your drey, or down to Monty?' I said.

'Hmm, I'll come down, looking at the acorn has made me feel hungry, and I know just the nut I want.'

'And you know where you've stored it?' I said.

Quiff stared at me, his eyes glinting, and exasperated he said, 'Of course I do' and raced down the tree.

When I hit solid ground a minute later, Quiff was scurrying around the undergrowth looking for his nut. Monty sat watching him and I walked over to him.

'I hear that Vincent is home? Monty said.

'Yes, in a cone' I said.

Monty chuckled and said 'He'll drive you mad.' He was quiet for a moment and said 'Did he tell you how he knew it was Retro that attacked him?'

'Yes, he said a small tabby called out his name, telling Retro that was enough' I said quietly.

Monty turned his face to me sharply and stared at me for a moment before looking away and watching Quiff. I had the feeling he wasn't really watching what Quiff was doing. 'So Vixen the vicious is back in the district. We have much to discuss at the Council meeting tonight' Monty said with a flint like glint in his eyes.

Chapter Nine

Mabel had left the building by the time I got home. Connie was back from her walk with Alex and looked more relaxed. She was in her sphinx pose watching Vincent who was in full throttle. He was scooping up ping pong balls with his cone, twirling them around until they shot out in different directions. At least he wasn't fighting the cone.

I sat next to Connie who said quietly 'I assume you've told Monty that Vixen is back.'

I nodded.

'How'd he take the news?'

'He was shocked but you know Monty, he keeps his thoughts and feelings hidden' I said.

Connie nodded and said 'I've been thinking.'

'Oh no, you haven't, have you?' I said trying to lift my spirits by teasing her.

'Hummph' Connie said 'Seriously, why would Vixen tell Retro to stop the attack on Vincent, it's not like her.'

'There's only one reason I can think of' I said.

Connie stared at me; her deep brown eyes troubled.

'To make sure that Vincent could tell us who attacked him' I said.

We watched Vincent launch another ping pong ball. It hit one of the dining chairs and rebound towards the window.

'But why?' Connie said.

'Why attack Vincent in the first place? Why call a stop? I don't know' I said.

'Hey what are you two muttering about?' Vincent said.

'I'm telling Connie that a Pursuit of the three men we've been looking for is taking place. I know I'm lying, but I don't want to worry Vincent, until I find out why he'd been beaten up.

'A real live Pursuit?' Vincent said.

'Yes, let's hope we have some success' I said.

'I want to be in the Pursuit' Vincent said petulantly.

'And you will, when you're old enough to be in the Cadets, but certainly not now, with or without a cone' Connie barked in a stern voice that brooked no argument. I knew that bark, given when she is worried, and says things louder than she should to hide her fear, not for herself, but for others, and this time, fear for Vincent.

Vincent blinked.

Anna must have heard Connie bark and came through from the shop.

'Hello you lot, keeping Vincent amused?' Anna said walking towards us whilst surveying the room which was littered with ping pong balls. She frowned at the dining chairs which were dislodged from their usual tidy stance under the table and shrugged. She bent down and gave Connie and I a quick snuggle, then strode over to Vincent and picked him up. He must have been taking lessons from Mabel, he did a very good ragdoll impression; going completely limp.

I could see Vincent's face under the cone; he wasn't happy and complained loudly. Even to an upright who doesn't speak feline, Vincent's meow was weighted with frustration. What he said I won't repeat; it certainly is not polite; I don't know where he's heard such language.

Anna checked her watch and said 'It's time for your first dose of medicine.'

We saw Vincent blink a few times and stare at us from under his cone.

'This is going to be interesting' I said.

'I bet it tastes nasty' Connie said.

'It always does' I said, nodding.

'Do you want any help? Alex said as his head popped in from the shop door.

'No, I'll be fine; how difficult can it be to give a wee little thing his meds.'

Anna glanced at us and said 'Don't worry you two, I'm not going to hurt him.'

I shook my head; we aren't worried about Vincent.

I watched as Anna attempted to get a pill into Vincent. Anna didn't use the oven gloves which was a mistake. He may be in a cone but he hasn't forgotten how to use his claws. When the direct approach didn't work, she tried tasty morsels of chicken and tuna which Vincent accepted as if he'd never eaten a thing in his life before, and then spat out the pill hidden in each morsel.

Anna seemed to be getting frustrated; a feeling Connie and I know well. She bought out the big guns – pilchards. I watched with a feeling of alarm; Anna's becoming as cunning as a cat. She crushed what was left of the pill into powder with two teaspoons and mixed the powder into a small morsel of the fish. She gave it to Vincent who ate it without complaint.

'I wonder how many times she's done that to you and me?' I said.

'I don't eat pilchards, nor do I make such a fuss' Connie said haughtily.

'No, you run and hide' I said.

Connie huffed, and turned, flinging her ears as only Connie can, she walked to Anna. She gently nudged her legs with her paw.

Anna bent down, gave Connie a stroke and said 'Hungry or Vincent driving you mad?'

'Yes to both' Connie yelped which I seconded, loudly.

Vincent isn't backwards in coming forward for his food. As soon as our bowls were put on the floor, he attacked his. Anna had raised his bowl off the floor so that his cone didn't prevent him from getting to it. I enjoyed my dinner and Connie whisked hers down too. I glanced over at Vincent who had gone very still, his cone covering his little bowl. Anna noticed too and gently picked him up; he was fast asleep. Whether it was the pills, a full tummy, ping pong hurling or the exertion of trying to rid himself of the cone; he'd worn himself out. Anna placed him in his bed, gently stroked him and headed for the shop door.

Connie wandered over to him and gently nudged him with her nose. 'He's almost angelic' she said.

'Hmm' I said.

'He doesn't need to know about Vixen' Connie said.

'I agree, there's no need to tell him, until we know more, and at least until he's out of his cone' I agreed.

'Only six more days to go.' Connie said.

Chapter Ten

Friday evenings are usually different to any other time of the week. I don't know if you feel the same way?

Connie and I stay clear of the pet gate on Fridays from around six o'clock. Anna and Alex take it in turns to grab something to eat from the kitchen whilst the one who isn't eating is manning the shop. This "in and out" is like a dance between them which goes on until closing at seven o'clock. A lot of customers also use the last hour before closing to hurry into the shop for wine, beer, soft fizzy drinks, chocolate and lottery tickets.

Alex also prepares for the Saturday morning deliveries of the newspapers. The sheets for the paper rounds listing who has what paper are printed and placed on the clip board, with the bills attached to them ready for the next morning when he builds the rounds. Before something you call social media, which Alex is on a lot, deliveries of newspapers used to happen every day of the week. The deliveries on week days fell to such small numbers that Alex himself delivers the few that are required for elderly people who can't get to the shop. It seems though, that everyone in the village wants their weekend papers delivered. The weekend papers are much thicker than weekday papers, with magazines and supplements that make them heavy. The paper boys and girls can't carry such weight, so Alex uses eight large trolleys to put the paper rounds in. As soon as the shop shuts at seven o'clock, as his last job, Alex brings the trolleys in from the garage and lines them up in the shop, ready for packing the rounds the next morning.

Alex then hurtles upstairs for a shower and a change of clothes whilst Anna takes Connie for a brief walk. As soon as Anna and Connie return, Anna takes a shower. I'm not sure why my uprights have the need to stand underneath artificial rain quite so much, but I must admit that both Alex and Anna smell fresh when they emerge again.

After the usual fuss of ensuring we have full water bowls and telling us to be "good" Anna is the first to leave. She picks up her art materials and the current canvass she's working on before calling to collect Esther. They both go to the same art group at the village hall. I don't know how much art gets done but at least it isn't being done anywhere near us and our fur.

Alex leaves straight after Anna. He usually carries a long thin metal case which has a cue in it. He likes to play snooker with his friends. Vincent hasn't worked out yet that the uprights playing snooker on the TV are real. He watches avidly when snooker is on, sitting right in front of the TV with his little head following each ball as it fires into pockets up and down the table. I haven't got the heart to tell him where Alex goes. He'd never be allowed near a snooker table anyway, so there's no point.

The house is very still and quiet. The door separating the shop from our home is locked, the TV isn't making a noise and neither Alex or

Anna are bustling about. Vincent is fast asleep looking angelic with the halo of the cone framing his face. Connie has slumped next to him and dozing.

I nudge her and her eyes force themselves open 'Hmm?'

'I'm going to the Council; I won't be long' I said.

Connie yawned and muttered something about keeping Vincent safe but had nodded off again before I reached the pet flap.

The evening air is fresh and I take a deep breath. My whiskers tell me there will be a frost, and hopefully the last of the year. I like spring; when the trees start to bud with fresh leaves and bluebells, snowdrops, and crocuses start to peep above ground. I like bluebells most of all, particularly when they carpet Dale Wood. I tend to go there once a year, always in the spring, with Quiff, who visits his cousins.

There's no point checking on Esther, she's gone to the art club with Anna. I walk down the garden to the bottom fence, leap onto it and fence walk the length of Mr Featherstone's garden. His buckets are neatly stacked. As the ribbon of tarmac is clear, I trot across it. I can see into the Desai's front living room window and they look cosy watching TV. I jog past their house and down into Monty's garden.

Monty is sitting with Jasper by the base of the lime tree and says hello. Jasper nods, I think I've mentioned he doesn't talk a lot.

Freddie, a large ginger tabby from the nearby estate is sitting next to Jasper. Freddie was born on a farm and likes to roam. We often see his picture on "Missing Freddie" posters plastered to lamp posts in the village put up by his uprights. They take them down again a few days later when he rolls home. He just likes to wander; you'd think they'd learn but Freddie says they're serial worry worts. He'd only been missing from home for one day last week before they started decorating the lamp posts with his picture. They'd probably be better living with a canine, it'd be best for their sanity as well as Freddie's.

Lunar, is in sphinx mode next to Freddie and says hello. Luna is a white British Short Haired with two splodges of ginger on her front paws and looks like she is wearing muddy boots all the time. She has the palest eyes I've ever seen in any being, thumbless or not. Her uprights are a busy young couple who've just had a baby girl. They live in the end terrace of quaint cottages at the edge of the village. I think her uprights named her well. She's out every night and all night. She's great at getting things done when there are clouds in the sky, but you've got next to no chance of asking her to Patrol or deliver a message if she can see the moon and stars. She just gets distracted, entranced by the sky above and often found gazing upwards.

March is the oldest and smallest cat amongst us. She is our district's Grand Elder. Her fur is black, like mine, but is showing signs of age with specks of grey. As Grand Elder, she knows the Cat Code inside out and backwards and what she decides is the law. She's teaching

Monty the finer points of the Cat Code, and, as her chosen successor, he'll be the next Grand Elder. She also asked Monty to train the cadets. She'll never admit it, but I think she asked Monty to give him a purpose after he lost his leg and became very down.

March's uprights, the Holmes, are in their early sixties and down to earth. They live in a large bungalow, with a long rear garden, that backs onto the school. March echoes her uprights with her no frills, straight to the point manner, but she can be very prickly. She doesn't allow fools anywhere near her, but she has always been fair.

When I was a kitten, the Grand Elder was Vixen. Vixen doesn't have a good heart or bone in her body. She is a feline Nasty and she twisted the Cat Code into her favour or for her cadets. Most of her cadets were vicious bullies and they were known as the VC's. The cadets who wouldn't accept her training were beaten and clawed by those that would. Monty was one of the cadets who refused to carry out her orders to drive out the village squirrels and was nearly clawed to death. Encouraged by Vixen, the cadets raided uprights' homes through open windows or unlocked pet doors and peed on carpets. The feline community, respecting the office of Grand Elder, lived with her rulings for a while, but banded together when it became clear that her orders were making a mockery of the Cat Code, and seriously damaging the reputation of felines. Vixen was deposed of her status as Grand Elder and driven out of the district, together with the cadets who remained loyal to her. Retro was the most vicious of her cadets and his infamy has grown with his tendency to keep returning. This time, he appears to be with Vixen.

Quiff was the last to join us, bouncing from his tree and landing gracefully next to Lunar. He'd brought a small nut with him for a snack, but held it behind his back and blinked when he caught March staring disapprovingly at him.

'We have enough members of the Council to begin. We have two matters that require attention. The attack on Vincent and the theft of items from Kinder, Esther Dickie' March said briskly.

I nodded, we all did.

'How is Vincent?' Quiff said.

'At home, recovering rapidly and the sooner he is out of his cone the better' I said.

'What's a cone?' Quiff said, hopping forward.

'It's like a hat without a top that your neck goes through, with the brim facing outwards. You can't see much, not even your feet, and you can't groom' Lunar said shuddering, looking at her feet and then up at the sky.

'That's awful, I wouldn't want a cone' Quiff said, bringing his nut forward and hugging it.

'Vincent will recover and that is what is important. Cones are put on thumbless beings for a reason and not because Vets are quirky' March said briskly.

I think Vets are quirky, but I wasn't going to argue with her.

Monty cleared his throat and said 'Claude, tell the Council what Vincent told you about the attack.'

I nodded, and said looking around the group, 'He told me he'd been attacked by Retro but I know he's never seen him; he's far too young. I asked him why he thought it was Retro, and he told me Retro stopped when a small tatty tabby ordered him to do so.'

March stared at me and nodded, taking the news without any visible sign of concern. The other cats gasped, and looked at each other, and Quiff's bushy tail trembled.

'We can't be sure the description of a small tabby is in fact Vixen, but Retro takes orders from no one but her, so we must assume it is' March said.

'But why is she back in the district, she knows she's not welcome or wanted?' Freddie said.

Everyone was silent and March said 'I don't know, but we will find out. I haven't been notified of any other attacks. Have there been any sightings of either of them since the attack on Vincent?'

I nudged Lunar who had looked up again at the moon. She gave me a startled look, and then after glancing around, nodded her thanks.

Freddie sat up from his sphinx pose and said 'I was at Green Farm yesterday. One of the chickens had been attacked and eaten. I didn't see Vixen, Retro or any of the V-C's but from the remains of the chicken, I'm pretty sure it was a feline attack and not a fox.'

'Do we have any reports of foxes in the area?' March said.

'Not at Green Farm. There is a skulk of foxes over in Dale Wood' Monty said.

'It may have been just a regular canine' Lunar said.

'From what Freddie has said it must either be a feline or fox' Monty said.

'Why do you say that?' Quiff said, his face furrowed.

'Foxes are the only type of canine that can retract their claws like a cat' I said.

'Oh, I never knew that' Quiff said.

'You've never been a cadet' I said.

Freddie shook his head and said 'it definitely wasn't a canine.'

March nodded and said 'There's a strong possibility that it's Vixen or Retro, but we need to be sure. The Cadets will patrol the

Kinders, and all adult felines will divert to Green Farm and areas surrounding the village which are not highly populated with uprights to find Vixen and Retro. Each search party will need to consist of at least two felines. Freddie, can you muster the adult cats from the estate to play their part?

'Yes, of course' Freddie said.

'If you locate them, I want them both brought to me. There is to be no challenge but, of course, defend yourselves if attacked in accordance with the Code' March said.

I nodded my agreement.

March looked at me intently and said 'Claude, you will not be involved in the search for them.'

I sprang up, and said 'But I want to …'

March interrupted me, her right front paw raised, and said 'Freddie and the rest of the adults will find Retro and Vixen. You are too close to the victim. I think Vincent has been targeted for a reason as there have been no reports of any other attack. I don't know why, but we shall find out. Until we do, you will not be part of the search for them. Your role is to keep Vincent safe. This is a direct order; is that understood?' March said firmly.

I sprang to my feet. This isn't fair! I want to be the one who finds Retro. He needs to learn beating up kittens has consequences. If I agree, and accept the order, I cannot break my promise; I'd be breaking faith with the Cat Code, be an outcast, and be known as someone without honour.

'I need your word that you will not search for them' March insisted.

I felt the hairs on my back spring up and my tail flicked in anger.

'Accept your orders Claude' Jasper said.

I stared at him, we all did, even Quiff dropped his nut. It's so rare for Jasper to say anything.

Jasper nodded, urging me to agree.

I sighed heavily, my tail still flicking in irritation.

'Your word Claude' March said briskly.

'I agree' I said, forcing out the words.

March stared at me intently. She has a way of making you feel that you've done something wrong, even when you know you haven't. I blinked first, to confirm my agreement, although seethed with frustration.

March nodded satisfied and said 'Turning to the Kinder, Esther Dickie, Monty has news of the Pursuit.'

Monty cleared his throat and said 'Yes, the people carrier headed towards the business park and as you know, we don't have the resources to follow it. However, the upright you call Trainers was dropped off at 85 Dale Road.'

I nodded, this was good news and I felt slightly mollified. 'Thank you, can you authorise a Spook on Trainers?' I said, looking at March.

March was silent for a moment and then said 'Yes, I'll sanction a Spook, but this issue needs resolving quickly; so ask the canines to get involved.'

I nodded. I may not be able to go to Green Farm or join in the search for Retro, but by all that was feline, I'd take solace by making Trainers' life a complete misery; he'd regret he ever broke into Esther's home.

Chapter Eleven

I'm stunned Connie agrees with the ruling of my exclusion from the search for Retro. I'm perplexed to say the least.

Connie told me to stop sulking (as if I've ever sulked) and urged me to tell her what else had been decided. She was delighted a Spook had been sanctioned and immediately hurtled through the pet door to start barking the news to other canines in the vicinity. I followed her outside and heard answering barks. I wanted to ask her why, by all that is feline, she was happy with banning me from the hunt for Retro. I was gearing up to put my point of view across, loudly, when Alex flung open the door and marched Connie back into the house.

I followed them as he looked grim which matched my mood.

'I don't know what's got into you?' Alex said in a tired exasperated voice with his hands on his hips looking down at Connie.

Connie wagged her tail tentatively and looked up at him with her soft brown eyes. He can't resist that look, to be fair, no one can.

Alex smiled, squatted onto his knees, and ran his hands gently down Connie's long silky ears shaking his head and said 'Anna will take you for a long run later but, until then, no … more … barking, its only 5.30!'

Connie wagged her tail fast; the universal canine way of saying she was happy.

Alex patted Connie's head, stood up and disappeared back into the shop.

'What's going on?' Vincent said sleepily from his basket.

'Nothing, go back to sleep, it's still early' I said.

Vincent yawned, shuffled around in his basket and closed his eyes.'

I watched him doze. Perhaps it isn't a good idea to discuss Retro anywhere near him. I thought about what March had said, about him being targeted, which worried me but, as Vincent is housebound with his cone, it's unlikely he's in immediate danger. I've decided not to talk to Connie anymore about Retro until I've had time to think. I don't want to fall out with her and said 'I'm off to spook Trainers.'

'Good luck' Connie said.

I'd been right, there was a frost and a good one. I breathed in the morning air and tingled with anticipation and the cold. Fence walking is slippery when its frosty so I jump over them instead, and trotted through gardens, all wearing frosty coats of white. It's pretty, but chilly on the paws. Anna has painted a snowy winter landscape of Dale Wood which hangs up in the hall. Vincent likes that painting, but he thought Anna hadn't coloured it in properly, until I explained it was a winter scene of snow. He's never seen snow and I've tried to explain what it's like and how thick it can get.

The odd bark from a canine can be heard; they are spreading the news of the Spook on the Target, Trainers.

Spooks don't happen often and wouldn't happen at all if uprights could speak feline or even canine. They are only carried out on Nasties and once the Nasty is identified they become what is known as the Target. It's rare for a Spook to be carried out to assist an upright, but we look after our Kinders and, when necessary, it is.

A good Spook, done properly and safely, as far as the canines are concerned, will bring the attention of good-natured uprights and Kinders to the Target. The best bit for me though will be to see Trainers spooked; he deserves to be.

The last Spook was carried out on a Nasty a few years ago. A great many felines gathered around his house and stayed there twenty-four hours of the day, every day, for as long as it took. We worked a rota system. Canines, who were walking with their uprights stopped in the street outside the property and sat, refusing to move, and barked. Frustrated uprights tried to drag, encourage with treats, or pick up their canines to move them along. Many of the canine uprights told Alex of the behaviour of their dogs when they visited the shop, and one of them told Anna she'd called the authorities about the number of cats surrounding the property, believing their dogs were barking at the cats. It didn't matter what the uprights believed; the Spook gave us what we wanted. A representative, who turned out to be a Kinder, from a local animal rescue centre arrived at the Nasty's property. No cat was caught, or in need of rescue, but the Kinder found a greyhound who had been badly treated. I won't upset you with the trauma of what she went through, but I can tell you, she now has a new name, Tulip, and living her best life with a family of uprights who adore her.

It took half an hour to get to 85 Dale Road; a small semi-detached house with a stone wall about four feet high to the front and side separating the garden from the one next door. I jumped onto the wall from the street and looked down at a small square garden. It hadn't been tended to for a while and was infested with frozen weeds and long grass; Esther would be horrified. I found a comfy, albeit cold spot, at the end of the wall knowing that Trainers would need to walk by me. Even if he was half asleep, he'd notice me.

Jasper silently jumped onto the wall and nodded hello. I nodded back. He'd brought along Peanut and Pickle who were very excited. Not many Cadets get to be involved in a real-life Spook, they train for it of course, but a live one is quite an event.

'Hello you two. I'd like you both on the side wall, together please, in hunting pose. Remember your training, say nothing and don't move a whisker. Most importantly focus your stares at him, and don't blink.'

They are a good pair and did exactly as they were told. Jasper positioned himself in the middle of the stone fence, facing the front door.

I don't know how long we are going to be waiting for Trainers to come out. I wish I'd had breakfast before leaving, but we'd stay in position until he appeared. We all focused on the front door and without looking at him I quietly said to Jasper 'Why did you advise me to agree to March's order at the Council last night.'

Jasper was silent, and I thought perhaps he hadn't heard me. I was about to repeat myself when Jasper said 'Retro won't allow himself to be found, he'll come out into the open when he's ready.'

'Oh, so you think it's useless to try to find him? I said.

Jasper nodded slowly and said 'Yes.'

I sighed and hoped Jasper was wrong. I pushed Retro to the back of my mind and focused my stare on Trainers' front door.

I calculated it was just after 7.00 am when Trainers emerged from his house. He clearly lived with someone, perhaps his Mother, as the sound of a TV or a radio blared from the open doorway for a moment before being silenced when he slammed the door shut. He was wearing his trainers, the same ripped jeans he wore when he broke into Esther's house and a grey hoodie. He had his back to me but turning, he did a double take when he spotted Peanut and Pickle on the side wall.

They were good. They didn't move a muscle and stared at him. Peanut managed to look cross and Pickle's longer fur stood on end making her look bigger than she is.

Trainers blinked first and strode towards them, his rat like face sneering with his arm raised. He stopped in his tracks when a very loud warning meow erupted from Jasper.

Trainers' head whipped around to look at Jasper and his eyes widened. I must admit Jasper has an imposing presence; he is a very big cat.

Trainers frowned, looked uncertain and dropped his arm. He backed away from Peanut and Pickle, keeping his eyes on Jasper. He turned and walked down the garden path towards me and stopped when he saw me.

In hunting stance, I stared at his rat like face. His eyes widened and he frowned looking uncertainly at me. He glanced across at Peanut, Pickle and Jasper and back to me.

We all continued to stare at him without moving a whisker.

I don't know whether he recognises me, but I hope he does.

He licked his thin lips and stepped forward slowly, keeping his eyes on me, as he edged out onto the pavement.

I turned. I knew that Jasper, Peanut and Pickle would turn too remaining in hunting stance. In unison, Jasper and I hissed at him loudly.

He stepped backwards and jumped when two dogs, a white Scottish Terrier and a Jack Russell who'd been approaching on their leads with their two elderly ladies sat down and started barking at him.

It's very important that canines sit and then bark when within four feet of a Target on a Spook; it preserves them from potential prosecution, or worse. Connie told me how difficult it is to sit and then bark. It took her hours to master.

I recognised the two elderly ladies. They both wear well made, low heeled sensible laced walking shoes. I think they are on their way to our shop as they are each carrying their shopping bags. They both looked confused and tried to urge their dogs to walk on. From what the ladies were saying the Scottish Terrier is called Jingle and the Jack Russell, Leo.

I nodded my thanks to the canines.

Trainers didn't say anything to the two elderly ladies. He backed away from them, and glancing furtively at me and Jasper, hurried up Dale Road towards the centre of the village.

Jingle and Leo stopped barking, stood up and pulled on their leads. The two elderly ladies were forced to walk faster as Jingle and Leo trotted after Trainers, barking intermittently, telling other canines where the Target was.

Trainers glanced back; he was clearly unnerved.

'Follow him' I said.

Peanut and Pickle took the high ground, walking along stone walls and fences, trailing after Trainers. Jingle and Leo, dragging their elderly uprights along were behind Trainers who was walking quickly. Jasper and I brought up the rear at ground level. It's rare that we cats walk together in this manner, but then again, it's rare for a Spook to take place.

In front of Trainers, and jogging towards us, I saw Duke the Doberman and his upright, the nice chap with the well-made trainers with a green tick on the side.

Jingle and Leo were good, but a dog the size of Duke suddenly stopping in front of Trainers, sitting down in the middle of the pavement, and issuing deep resonant 'Target Here' barks is imposing.

Duke's person was a bit perplexed by Duke's behaviour and urged him up and on.

Duke ignored him and continued to sit, barking at Trainers who was edging around Duke by plastering his back against a front garden fence wall.

'Sorry, I don't know what's got into him' Duke's upright said.

'You should keep that thing on a leash!' Trainers snapped.

'He's not hurting you, with his bottom planted on the floor' Duke's upright said exasperated.

Trainers spat on the ground and, having edged around Duke, who continued to bark and watch him, Trainers glanced back at us all, and hurried on, picking up his pace.

Duke stood up and politely moved out of the path for Jingle, Leo and their two elderly ladies.

I heard Duke's upright say 'I've never known Duke do that before, it's most odd.'

'Jingle and Leo here did exactly the same thing when they saw that young man. He must be a bad one, animals know you know' Jingle's upright said.

Duke's upright nodded and looked at the retreating figure of Trainers. He looked thoughtful and said 'They do don't they.'

I nodded at Duke, who raised his eyebrows at me, in quiet and shared exasperation.

Chapter Twelve

The advantage of involving canines in a Spook when the Target is moving is that we always know where the Target is. This gives every thumbless being in the vicinity the opportunity to get involved. Felines balance on front fences or sit on car bonnets and stare at the Target, hissing as he walks by. Canines who can get out of their homes, sprint to their garden gates, or sit at the edge of their upright's property and bark as he passes. Canines walking with their uprights, who are either half asleep or looking at their mobile phones, are jerked to a standstill by their canine suddenly sitting down and barking at Trainers as he approaches.

It's a lot of attention on a Target. When spooked enough, the natural reaction of a moving Target is to speed up. Trainers is no different and begins to run.

I know some uprights like to run, wearing the appropriate clothing, like Anna. As running is such a regular occurrence, uprights and us thumbless beings don't bat as much as an eyelid. However, it's noticed by everyone when an upright is being chased by a canine.

Urgent barks telling the canine to stop chasing the Target echo back to me. Trainers is out of sight having turned a corner, but from what the canines are saying I know he's on Amble Road. I look at Jasper and, worried, we both set off towards Trainers' location.

We take a more direct route through gardens and over fences.

The dis-advantage of a Spook involving canines with a running Target is that it can get out of hand. Canines are trained not to chase a Target for their own protection, but young canines caught up in the excitement can forget their training.

Jasper and I are making good headway and I'm listening to the continued barks but feel a chill run down my spine when I hear that Bailey, a Tibetan Mastiff, started the chase.

Bailey is enormous with a body weight of about 80 lbs. She looks bigger due to the amount of fur she has. She's a very gentle soul who is very protective of her upright, Fiona. The good news is she isn't known for running fast or far and she'll soon slow down.

Jasper and I landed on the tarmac of Amble Road and stopped.

This is a serious situation for Bailey.

Trainers had climbed into one of the trees that line Amble Road. It's not a particularly big tree and Quiff wouldn't give it a second glance but a tree big enough to allow Trainers to climb high. Bailey stood below the tree, panting, her tongue long and peering up at him. Trainers was swearing and cursing her but her response was to sit down and continue to stare.

Other dogs I recognised from the Village, with leads trailing, having jerked free from their uprights' hands joined her. They all mingled around the bottom of the tree. Some put their front paws onto the tree trunk and looked up at Trainers, panting and barking at him.

'We need to sort this out and form a crowd; there isn't a grown up amongst them. Uprights need to see these canines are not dangerous' I said.

Jasper is fully aware of our theory to crowd with good behaviour. We've never put it into practice, but I hope it will work.

Jasper nodded, and we sprinted over. Jasper silently and calmly sat in front of Bailey.

I stood as tall as I can and shouted 'Canines, stop! Sit down, and don't say anything more or move. Your behaviour needs to be pristine; you will be seen as a pack!'

The young canines looked at me, looked at one another and finally realising the enormity of their chase planted their bottoms on the ground. I nodded, satisfied, and sat next to Bailey.

A large branch of dead wood hurtled down towards us. Trainers had clearly torn it from the tree. The branch didn't hit anyone. I looked up and stared at Trainers who glared back.

One of the young canines, I think her name is Dolly, a Cockerpoo, leapt to her feet and barked at him.

'Stop! I shouted and gave Dolly one of the stares I reserve for Vincent when he's being a brat. She blinked and sat down.

I sat next to Bailey and looked up at her. Even sitting, Bailey's head is a long way above mine. 'Why on earth did you start a chase' I said.

Bailey looked down at me, her eyes mournful. She sighed and said 'I'm sorry, I just ... forgot I shouldn't chase. He wasn't nice to Fiona and he spat at her ... and well he's just such a ... Nasty isn't he.'

I couldn't argue with that.

Bailey's upright, Fiona, arrived wearing well-worn brown leather walking boots. She is a small, very thin middle-aged woman with a red face and greying hair. Her woolly hat was clinging to her head and she looked completely baffled and out of breath. The other canine's uprights arrived behind her looking equally confused, some angry, but all relieved their canine had at least stopped.

I heard the familiar trundling wheels of a paper delivery trolley on the pavement behind me and glancing back saw Tommy Drummond. Tommy is always the first to arrive on a Saturday morning for his trolley and is a very efficient delivery person. Alex is always saying Tommy has a good work ethic and will go far. I don't know what a "good work ethic" means but I hope he doesn't go too far; I'd miss him if he did. I've known him all my life. When he was younger, on odd occasions, he used to play with me at home after he'd finished school when his Mum or Dad couldn't pick him up until later. He used to have a miniature torch which he shone on the walls for me. I used to love to try to catch the light. I realised I never would, but it was good training for agility.

'What's going on?' Tommy said.

Fiona picked up Bailey's lead and turning to Tommy said 'Bailey ran after that man in the tree. Other dogs followed and here we are.'

'Get that bloody thing away from me' Trainers shouted.

'She won't hurt you' Tommy shouted back and moving forward, stroked Bailey's head.

We all looked up at Trainers, feline, canine and uprights alike. He's very rattled.

A young Labrador's upright, an elderly man wearing black lace up shoes, holding a walking stick and wearing a blue flat cap shouted 'For goodness sake, come down, you're the one making a fuss!'

Fiona grabbed Bailey's harness and encouraged her to move. Bailey glanced down at me and I shook my head. Fiona started to tug at her harness. Bailey's body weight is far more than Fiona's and she doesn't stand any chance of budging her.

'Oh, shut up old man, what do you know!' Trainers sneered.

'Well really. The young people of today' which started a debate amongst the uprights who were beginning to lose whatever sympathy they may have had for Trainers.

This couldn't be better.

Peanut and Pickle arrived and looked across at me.

I nodded to them both and asked if they would sit either side Dolly, pointing a stern face at Dolly who was twitching. She was finding it difficult to stay still and keep her bottom on the ground. Hopefully Peanut and Pickle would help her focus.

Some of the uprights tried to encourage their canines to move along, with promises of treats when they got home. No canine moved. We thumbless beings continue to sit like statues, staring up at Trainers who looked increasingly uncomfortable on his branch.

Ida Morris, with her paper folded and stuffed down one Wellington boot and the supplements and magazine in the other marched up to us. She still has a forthright manner of a Head Teacher although she retired some years ago. She glanced around, and then looked up into the tree. As it's still not spring, there are no leaves on the tree and Trainers can be seen very clearly.

'What's going on?' Anna's voice said. She appeared at the side of the crowd and stood next to Ida Morris. I turned my head and she spotted me and raised her eyebrows. They went even higher when Connie trotted over to me, her lead extending from the anchor point on Anna's waist, and sat down beside me.

Connie's tongue was long and she was panting, her breath warm and said 'I've never seen a Spook like this.'

'No, we've gone from Spook, to Chase to Crowding. Hopefully no canine will be considered dangerous if they all stay still and behave themselves.'

'That's just a theory, will it work?' Connie said.

'It's all we've got' I said.

Fiona was looking harassed, and told Anna and Ida what had happened and continued, 'Bailey's such a gentle dog despite her size, and it's most unlike her to run … well … anywhere. He wasn't particularly nice to me when she just plonked herself down and sat barking at him, but even so, I can't tell you how awful I felt when she just started chasing him.'

Ida frowned and said 'Mmm, Bailey probably didn't like his attitude towards you, but that doesn't explain why all the other dogs and look, goodness me, the cats, are sitting staring at him.'

'Yes, but he won't come down and none of them will move!' Fiona said.

'This is very odd behaviour' Ida said frowning.

'Do you mean it's odd that he's is in a tree or all these animals are sat looking at him?' Tommy said.

'Both, but we can't stand here all day. I'll get home and call the police!' Ida said loudly.

'No! I don't want the police here, you stupid old bat. Just go away, all of you and take your flea-bitten mongrels and moggies with you!' Trainers yelled.

Anna looked at Ida, and frowning said 'No need to go home Ida, I'll call them. I have my mobile with me.' Anna unstrapped the phone from her arm band and dialled.

Trainers looked angry and started swearing, language which I'm not going to belittle myself to repeat. March told me once that Nasties often use this type of language because they don't know many words or have limited intelligence and can only express themselves in this way.

People who had attempted to urge their canines away stopped and started chatting to each other. The crowd had grown since we first arrived, some uprights don't even have a canine with them. I know you are like us, curious, well who wouldn't be with a man in a tree surrounded by well-behaved but immovable thumbless beings.

Between the legs of the uprights, it wasn't long before I saw a police patrol carrier arrive and stop. The two front doors opened and two pairs of solid black boots belonging to a very young police officer and Sergeant Wisby got out and strode towards us.

The crowd parted to allow Sergeant Wisby to stand near the bottom of the tree. He had a good look up at Trainers and glanced around the multiple canines and felines sat quietly watching Trainers. He nodded at Anna and his impressive eyebrows rose slightly when he spotted me sandwiched between Connie and Bailey with Jasper in front of her.

Sergeant Wisby took his hat off and shouted to Trainers 'I suggest you climb down immediately young man.'

'No! I'm not moving until you clear all these ruddy dogs away, and particularly that great bear of a dog; that's vicious that is!' Trainers spat, pointing at Bailey.

'Lie down Bailey' I whispered.

Bailey looked at Sergeant Wisby and slowly lay down into sphinx pose.

Sergeant Wisby took a pace or two and squatted in front of Jasper and Bailey. Bailey looked up at him and he stroked her head. He smiled and stood up. He turned back to Trainers and said 'That dog is not vicious, you're the one causing a nuisance, climb down now.'

Trainers looked mutinous. His rat like face tight with tension, his thin lips looked like a squiggly line.

'Come on, get down here, you'll be quite safe, nothing's going to hurt you' Sergeant Wisby said.

Trainers began to move slowly. He certainly isn't a climber; his foot placement and sense of balance is diabolical, but he was at least coming down.

I hadn't seen Quiff arrive. He must have got here leaping along the line of trees on Amble Road, using the top branches, but he made an appearance now, as he jumped onto the branch Trainer's was holding and shouted 'Aha!'

Startled, Trainers swore, lost his grip and grabbed at the nearest branch, missed and somehow ended up swinging from his knees, upside down. Everyone gasped, and it is a measure of how much goodwill there is in uprights and thumbless beings; no one wanted to see Trainers fall and hurt himself.

Trainers was visibly shaken, and his face was an odd grey colour.

I've sometimes struggled with gravity, particularly when I was a kitten, but sometimes gravity can be a wonderful thing, particularly when it comes to Trainer's pockets. His phone, a few coins and two small crystal swans fell from them and hit the grass beneath the tree.

'Hey, they look like Esther Dickie's swans!' Anna shouted, immediately pointing at them, as the crystals lay glinting in the sunlight.

Ida took a step forward, and peering at the swans said 'I think you're right.'

'No, they belong to my … my…. Aunt!' Trainers stuttered sounding desperate. He gulped rapidly, his face turning an interesting shade of puce.

Sergeant Wisby stepped towards the items in the grass and asked his Constable to assist Trainers down. Whilst the Constable was busy with Trainers, Sergeant Wisby produced pale blue gloves, blew in them, put them on and bending down picked up the two swans and put them in two separate small clear bags which he sealed. He then collected the phone and coins, popping those into separate bags and stood up.

'You'll come along with me to the Station' Sergeant Wisby said as soon as Trainers was on the ground and upright.

'But … why, they are my Aunts, I've done nothing wrong!' Trainers spat.

I'd frankly had enough. 'No, you're a Nasty lying thief !' I shouted. It came out as a screech-come-meow but it made Trainers jump and he shrank behind Sergeant Wisby. No person understood me of course, no one speaks feline, but I felt better.

'Have you seen this cat before?' Sergeant Wisby asked Trainers.

'Yes, it's a pest, that's what it is!' Trainers shouted.

Connie lept to her feet and the other canines followed.

Sergeant Wisby looked at all the thumbless beings, frowning, and stared at me. I blinked at him. I hope he was remembering that Anna told him; I was at Esther's home when the theft took place.

'Come with me young man, and we'll sort this out' Sergeant Wisby said firmly taking Trainer's arm and walked to the police carrier.

Trainers tried to shrug Sergeant Wisby away, cursing and complaining that he was the one that had been picked on by a bunch of flea-bitten animals.

Sergeant Wisby ignored him. Having put Trainers in the back seat of the police carrier, Sergeant Wisby turned to us all and said 'Can you each give your names to the Constable before leaving. We may need to speak to you at some point.'

Chapter Thirteen

One of the many benefits of being feline is that we don't have to stand in line with our uprights. We can just melt away. Jasper nodded goodbye and Peanut and Pickle scampered up the tree after Quiff. I didn't know whether he was still there but I'd thank him later. Anna was giving her name to the Constable and Connie said she'd see me at home as I walked past her.

Having had very little sleep since the Council meeting last night, and with no breakfast, a meal I rarely miss, I was very tired and hungry. Determination and patience had kept me going during the Spook, fear for Bailey had driven me during the chase and crowding, but now I just want to eat and sleep. I doubt I'll be given the opportunity to even have a nap when I get home; Vincent and Connie will want to know every detail.

I take the direct route home through gardens and realise I've missed Saturday morning at the shop. There's always a buzz early on Saturdays and Sundays, when the young uprights turn up to collect their trolleys to deliver the papers.

Unless it's raining on Saturday and Sunday mornings, I sit outside, in the large planter that stands between the two doors to the house and the shop. It always has a bay tree in the centre of it that gets dressed with lights in the winter. In the spring Anna, with help from Esther, surrounds the bay tree by planting it with flowers. They have both learnt from previous flattened flowers that there is a particular spot where I like to sit. This gives me a good view of the comings and goings of the young uprights who deliver the papers.

I cheer myself up with the thought of tomorrow, Sunday morning, I can see all the young uprights then.

At home, I find Vincent and Mabel are amusing themselves with ping pong twirling. There are ping pong balls everywhere. Vincent has got it down to a fine art; scoop, twirl and flick. Once the ping pong ball is launched, Mabel tries to hit it. She's missing most of them but, to be fair, it's hard to judge which way the ball will fly out of the cone.

'Uncle Claude!' Mable said as she spotted me mid leap.

Vincent lowered his cone and looked at me. He turned his head to one side and the ping pong ball that had been in his cone dribbled out and rolled away.

Mabel bounced over to me and said 'Uncle Claude, tell us about the Spook! Where is it now? When will it finish? What's the target doing ....'

'No Mabel, shut up! Vincent said looking at me intently as he walked towards me. He looked up and stared into my eyes. I have to say this is most disconcerting. I must be tired; I blinked first.

'Claude needs to rest.' Vincent said matter of factly.

'But I want to know ....' Mabel said.

Vincent turned towards her and she stuttered to silence. He turned back to me and said 'I saved your breakfast from Mabel and Connie.'

I must admit I am stunned. Vincent thinking of others before himself and his own curiosity? Is this a grown-up version of Vincent? When did that happen or am I so tired I'm no longer thinking straight? I nodded my appreciation, walked to my bowl, ate, drank some water which was refreshing, wandered into the sitting room, and landed in the middle of the evil rug.

*****

I was chasing Retro in my dreams, but just as I got to him, he disappeared into one of Mr Featherstone's buckets which were scattered surrounding me. I surfaced from this frustrating dream to the sound of Vincent's worried voice and heard him say 'But ... he's been asleep now for such a long time.'

'Because he was very tired' Connie said, a tinge of exasperation in her voice.

'I know that, but I tell you; it's the rug. If he'd gone to sleep anywhere else, he'd be awake by now!'

'Well, it's comfy. No one stays asleep unless they are comfy' Connie said.

'That's the point, it's too comfy to be any good for you. What if it's so comfy he never wants to leave it? Vincent said.

I opened my eyes and blinked at them. Connie was in sphinx pose at right angles to me on the rug, and Vincent was in hunting pose at the very edge of it, staring at me.

'There you are, look, he's awake!' Connie said.

'Claude, you must get off the rug, it's made you sleep for hours. You'll only go to sleep again and never wake up if you stay on it' Vincent said, a note of urgency in his voice.

I yawned. The open curtains told me it was late, as it was dark outside, but as Anna and Alex were not in the sitting room, the shop hadn't closed, so it was before 7 pm.

'I stood up, and stretching said 'Have I missed dinner?'

'Yours is waiting for you in the kitchen' Connie said.

'Good, I'll have a bite to eat, and tell you what happened in the Spook'.

'Oh, there's no need, we've pieced it all together' Connie said with Vincent nodding, his cone gently bashing the rug.

'How?' I asked.

'Everyone that comes into the shop is talking about it' Vincent said.

'You mean about Trainers in the tree?' I said.

'Yes, and about Bailey chasing him, but mainly about the silent crowding. You've been mentioned a few times too' Connie said.

This isn't good news; far from it!

'What's wrong?' Vincent said.

'We need a plan' I said.

'Why?' Vincent said.

'We can't have uprights thinking thumbless beings are intelligent and work together' I said.

'But we do, all the time' Vincent said.

'I know, you know, Connie and the canines know, all thumbless beings know, but we don't want uprights to know. Now that they know, or think they do, we need to stop such thoughts from their minds' I said.

'But I say hello to my friends when we go walking, and uprights don't mind that, why would it matter if they knew we actually have our own Code and community' Connie said baffled.

'A quick hello to a friend, even playing chase or with a ball thrown by an upright is one thing; that's expected. An organised group of thumbless beings is quite another' I said.

'I don't think the Kinders would mind' Vincent said thoughtfully.

'Probably not, but the world isn't made up of Kinders, there are Nasties out there' I said.

'What could a Nasty do?' Vincent said.

'I don't know; I don't think like a Nasty but it wouldn't be good for us.'

'I'm pretty sure it's no worse than it is now and you are worrying about nothing' Connie said firmly.

'I'm going to talk to Monty' I said.

Vincent's eyes widened, and he watched me carefully, and then looked at the rug, a satisfied look on his face as I walked by him. I heard him say to Connie 'He's escaped the rug this time, but who's to say he won't next time, or you for that matter Connie, you've got to be so careful.'

I left Connie trying, once again, to explain that the rug was nothing more than a rug, and dashed over to Monty's.

I found him sitting with March, behind one of the various conifers dotted along the boundary of his garden.

'Hello Claude' Monty said.

March nodded and said "The Spook gave a good result, probably the best we've achieved with the upright, Trainers, being taken away by the police.'

'Yes, let's hope that Sergeant Wisby can piece together Trainer's involvement with the theft' I said nodding.

'It's a pity that the young canine Bailey gave chase' Monty said.

'I believe Duke will be increasing the young canine training programme. To be fair to Duke, there are a lot of young dogs in the Village. With the canine Elders not having the freedom to see them often, it must be difficult to train them effectively' March said.

I hadn't thought of that. Thinking about Connie, she was never allowed out of the garden on her own without Anna or Alex. I couldn't recall how she was trained for Spooks, but I'd ask her later.

I cleared my throat and said 'I'm here because we may have a problem.'

Monty and March looked at me intently.

'Connie and Vincent tell me that the uprights coming into the shop are talking about Trainers in his tree, but the focus is on the crowd we all formed to protect Bailey.'

'I understand that you took control of the crowd, is that right? Monty said.

'Well, ...yes, all the chasers were young canines, and I was worried that uprights would take Bailey as a dangerous dog and leader of a pack. I should have allowed an occasional bark, but I wasn't thinking beyond saving Bailey' I said.

'It's possible uprights have caught on that we are more intelligent than they thought' Monty said.

'Hmmm, I'm not too concerned. The upright's grapevine will help of course, but I'll send an alert to Duke. He'll tell the canines to behave as their uprights would expect for a time. Leave that with me, and let me consider further' March said, and peering at me muttered 'You have presented me with an interesting course of action.'

'You'll also need to behave as your uprights would expect for a time' Monty said.

I nodded and said 'Yes of course, but how will the grapevine help?

Monty chuckled and looked at March.

March's eyes gleamed, and said 'It's fascinating, but uprights aren't like felines with our whispers. Our whispers to each other stay the same, or even shortened sometimes by lazy cats. Uprights add to a story they hear, and when told to the next upright, the story grows. What you are left with, is a story so out of proportion to what actually happened, the original story becomes lost and forgotten.'

'Let's hope the grapevine is working as it should' Monty said.

'There's no reason to suggest it won't' March said.

It seemed wrong that stories grew like that, but I shook my head and said 'Any news on Retro?'

'No, there's been no sightings of Vixen, Retro or the V'C's, they've got themselves a good hiding place' Monty said.

'He'll be found soon, but you are not to search; my order still stands' March said.

I nodded reluctantly, and said 'Is Quiff at home?'

'He's out and about around the village' Monty said.

'I'll need to thank him for scaring Trainers, his timing was perfect' I said.

'I'll let him know you are looking for him, but now go and behave like a cat' Monty said.

On my way home, I called in Esther's garden, did a sweep of it, and jumped onto the kitchen window sill. A new window had been installed, a solid one that wasn't made of wood. No one using a palette, or any other type of knife, would get into this one. I peered in and saw Esther sitting with Anna and Ida at the kitchen table. They were sharing a bottle of red wine, their half full glasses glinting in the light and sitting amongst a lot of paint tubes. Oil and acrylic paint oozed on their palettes, and brushes littered the table.

I shuddered at the memory of oil paint in my fur and on my paws. I'd walked through oils on a canvass left to dry on the kitchen table when I was a kitten, which got stuck in my fur when I groomed. Anna still has the painting of my paw prints, which she says "adds" to it.

I still remember the vegetable oil, soap, and the water that she used to get the paint off my paws and fur. It was the last time I've been in the bathroom. It has a large, deep tub in it which gets filled with water, like an indoor pond. The bath wasn't pleasant for me or my uprights. Alex held me whilst Anna scrubbed. I then got buried in a large towel, and vigorously rubbed dry, although I don't know who was the wettest, me, Alex or Anna.

Anna and Alex are not aware that I'd nearly drowned, in a canvass bag thrown into the river, when I was very young, by what I now know was a Nasty.

Esther still looks like the stuffing has been pulled out of her. Her face is quite grey but there is a ghost of a smile as she listens to Anna talking. I can't hear what Anna is saying, this window is very well fitted. A glass of wine and Anna's company will do her good. I'm not so sure about Ida's company though, I haven't had much to do with her, and I wondered idly whether she wore her wellingtons indoors. I may have night vision but I can't see through a wooden table and left them to it.

Chapter Fourteen

I'm sitting outside, in the plant pot housing the olive tree, with one eye on the sky, crowded with large grey clouds, bulging with water. Tommy Drummond smiles at me as he briskly walks into the shop for his paper delivery sheet. He's always cheerful, even early on Sunday morning.

Tommy wanted to be a paper delivery boy for ages, but no one is allowed to be until the age of thirteen. He likes to spend the money he earns on his hobby, music and playing the guitar. He talks to Alex a lot about music and apparently, he's always breaking his guitar strings. He's saving up for an amplifier to make a louder noise. I hope by the time he gets his amplifier; he can play something that sounds like music, rather than the noise he listens to (we all do) when near his home. I've been told the music is "heavy rock" which is a pretty good description; it sounds like heavy rocks falling, so I'm not sure why a guitar is needed?

Tommy set off with his trolley. Seven more trolleys, clad in fluorescent yellow jackets packed with papers would leave within the hour, when the other paper delivery boys and girls arrived. I don't think any of them will turn into Nasties as they grow, but whether they will be Kinders remains to be seen.

When a newby starts, Alex goes with them, to make sure they know where they are going and how to read the paper delivery sheet. Sometimes a trolley arrives back with an odd paper inside which should have been delivered. On rare occasions, the wrong paper goes to the wrong house, which can happen when the paper delivery upright is half asleep. I can't say I blame them; uprights really do need to be fully-fledged larks to do the job. I sometimes follow a newby, keeping out of sight of course, just to make sure they are on the right track.

The shop is open until noon today as it's Sunday. After I've watched the last trolley trundle off, I breakfast and spend most of the morning by the gate to the shop where I can study shoes with an occasional doze. Today, unusually, Vincent joined me and I had been teaching him about shoe sizing. He got bored and has found shredding magazines with his claws a newly found way to pass the time. He can't see the results until he moves away but it's beginning to look like he's making a good job of creating confetti. Connie has gone with Anna for a long run and won't see the effect of Vincent's work until she gets back.

There are a lot of shoes I recognise. They are regular customers to the shop, and the early risers comment to Alex that they've heard I'm one of the felines who sat with the canines whilst Trainers was in his tree. Most can't believe the canines didn't chase me. Without knowing, Alex has the perfect answer. He didn't know where I was yesterday morning, but, if I was one of the cats it would make sense, as I live with a dog. That seems to satisfy the early risers but by late morning the story of Trainers in his tree had grown to something unrecognisable. Apparently, Trainers is a known thief; some of the dogs were his, and were waiting for his command to attack the felines who'd been surrounded. I think this is what March meant about the grapevine.

A pair of high heeled, tan leather, pointed toe stilettoes appear in my line of vision and walk to the counter. I've always been a bit wary of stilettoes, the heel could cause some serious damage to thumbless beings. As uprights don't have particularly great balance, I've always been rather impressed how you can totter around on points no bigger than your little finger nail, and how your feet can fit into shoes that are so pointed at the front. Perhaps your feet grow into them, a bit like Vincent growing into his fur?

Stilettoes is wearing a long beige coat to match her shoes and handbag, and very smart she looks too. Her head appears above the counter top. She has long chestnut hair and large laughing brown eyes. I like her; she has even features. She'd be a British Shorthaired if she were a cat.

'Hello, can I help you' Alex said.

Stilettoes says hello and asks for two bottles of Merlot.

Alex smiles, I think he likes her too, and produces two bottles of red wine from the shelving behind him, and placing them on the counter said "There you are, is there anything else?'

'Oh, what a gorgeous cat' Stilettoes said, peering down at me with a slight smile, and a bit of a twinkle in her eye.

'Thank you' I said.

Alex glances down at me, stretches over the pet gate, gives my head a stroke (a bit embarrassing) and said 'Yes, Claude is a rather handsome boy, but don't set him off, he can become quite vocal.'

I think Alex is trying to say I talk too much!

'We give check-ups for a lot of black cats handed in at the sanctuary for re-homing. A lot of people still think an entirely black cat is unlucky or a bad omen' Stilettoes said.

I'm not sure how to take this?

Alex said, sounding surprised 'What? People don't still believe in witchcraft, do they?'

'I don't know what it is, but it wouldn't surprise me. I had a black cat once, she was totally loyal to me and I'm tempted to get another, but I'm so busy at the surgery, it wouldn't be fair' Stilettoes said.

'Are you a doctor?' Alex asks politely.

'Of sorts, I'm a Vet' Stilettoes said.

Immediate movement is required but, if I go, it'll look like I've understood she's a Vet which isn't ordinary cat behaviour. I make myself remain. I'm ruffled to say the least. How can smiling eyes Stilettoes be a Vet? Why isn't she in a white coat and smelling of disinfectant?

I watch her warily through the gate as she continues to chat to Alex and picks up a newspaper from the rack, chocolate from the confectionary shelves and pays Alex. She's probably not local as she doesn't mention the story about Trainers, which is a relief.

'See you soon little man' Stilettoes says to me smiling as she picks up her items.

I blink, what does she mean? I won't be seeing her or any other Vet any time soon.

I don't have time to think about it. The front door to the house burst open, and Connie thunders towards me along the hall, still attached to her extendable lead, her tongue long and shouts 'Claude, Retro's got Quiff!'

'Where?' I said standing up.

'Near the bandstand at the park, I tried to intervene but Anna wouldn't stop and I was dragged away. I've been barking out his location all the way here, but I'm not sure anyone is listening' Connie shouted.

'That's enough Connie! For goodness sake, stop barking and calm down!' Anna said gasping for breath.

Alex stuck his head through the door, looked at Anna, and said 'Where's the fire, you okay?'

'I will be, when I've caught my breath. I had to be very firm with Connie; she wouldn't leave the park, and then she literally dragged me back here. I don't know what's got into her' Anna gasped.

I touched Connie's nose in thanks. I don't really care whether Alex and Anna think this is correct cat behaviour or not. I sprinted to the pet door, passing Vincent surrounded by heaps of torn paper.

Connie shouted 'Be careful!'

I startled Mabel as she was heading towards the pet door and hurriedly told her to stay indoors with Vincent.

Victoria Park is an open green space on two levels. The lower level is the Cricket Club with a cricket pitch and a pavilion near the people carrier park. When cricket isn't being played in the summer, the pitch is used by uprights strolling, with or without canines, or for football. The upper level has a small play park for younger uprights with swings, slides, a see saw and climbing frame. I must admit the slide is fun; I go on it occasionally, at night when uprights are asleep, and no one else is watching.

The upper level also has tarmacked paths which surround flower beds planted by the local authority, and benches are dotted everywhere. Most of the benches form a ring around the band stand which is very old. The band stand is round and is made of iron. It has a raised wooden floor, ornate iron work, to stop uprights falling off, and a roof. In the summer evenings, when it's hot, the village brass band sit in it and play tunes for a few hours. When the music is playing, the benches are busy with uprights coming and going. Some uprights even bring brightly coloured checked blankets which they lay on the grass and sit on to have picnics, shaded beneath the branches of the many trees.

The Park may be busy in the summer but now, it's grey and cheerless. The light is dimming with swollen heavy clouds and huge blobs of rain are beginning to fall, splattering like eggs as they hit the ground. The feeling of cold water penetrates my fur and I shiver, my instinct is to seek cover but I race forward, worried about my friend Quiff. I quickly scan the cricket ground from the upper level as I sprint to the bandstand. A group of young uprights are playing football, and the fitness club who run and squat around the edge of the cricket pitch is finishing.

The rain is coming down fast, in sheets of water, and thunders against the roof of the band stand. It's been about fifteen minutes since Connie spotted Quiff, dragged Anna back home and for me to get here.

Gasping for breath, I leap onto the band stand railing to get a better view and start to pace around it. It gives me a good ariel view of the whole park. I see the uprights from the fitness club running to the people carrier park, and the footballers run for shelter under the cricket pavilion.

Moving around the railing, I spot Quiff. He is on the ground and hunched up, constantly turning around, surrounded by three felines. I don't recognise the ginger tabby nor the grey and white, but I recognise Retro with his thick brown and tan coat.

Quiff is small against the three cats surrounding him. He's soaked, and his tail is sodden with mud. He's trying to get away, but each time he moves, one of the cats' heads him off with outstretched claws, swiping at him.

'Hey! Leave him alone!' I shouted, leaping off the band stand rail. I wade through puddles that are forming. The icy rain is falling heavily and penetrates my fur. The familiar memory of cold water over my head, soaking in and sucking me down in the river with the bag clinging around me, is all I can see and feel for a few moments. I shake my head, and force the memory away. I focus on Quiff; he needs my help.

Retro turns to face me, his wet tail flicking like a snake. He has a scar across his nose and one of his ears is tatty, possibly shredded in one of his many fights.

I stop near him, but not too close to allow him to jump on me.

Retro says nothing but stares at me with his pale yellow eyes.

I stare back, he blinks first, looks away and casually walks towards me.

'Well, well, well, you're Claude, aren't you?' Retro said.

'Yes, but who I am is not relevant.'

'Oh but it is, you are a law-abiding member of March's Council' Retro said.

'That's right' I said flicking my tail in annoyance 'So, what if I am?'

'I've heard the whispers ... you've got orders not to search for me.'

'When have you been bothered about what March orders, you don't even recognise her as a Grand Elder' I said.

'True ... but ... you do' Retro said, his eyes gleaming in triumph.

I stared at him.

'Now you've found me, you may as well have a go at taking your revenge for little Vincent, I know it's what you want' Retro sneered.

I kept my anger within and walked to the right. Retro walked to the left, and we started to circle each other.

Every whisker, muscle and piece of my wet fur wanted to hurt Retro. I'm not afraid of him, but I held back; something isn't quite right. How would he know Vincent is a member of my family? Why is he boasting about hurting him? It's as if he wants me to attack him, but why?

We continued to circle, eyeing each other up. Out of the corner of my eye, I can see that the ginger and grey and white cats aren't paying as much attention to Quiff, but every time Quiff moves, they are both there, with their claws out, keeping him exactly where he is.

I stopped dead in my tracks. My whiskers didn't wiggle, they twanged, remembering what Jasper had said. I started to walk again, my wet fur feeling heavy.

Retro matched my step, always directly opposite.

'Of course, I haven't broken my orders from March' I said.

'What do you mean, you're here aren't you' Retro sneered.

'I was told you had Quiff.'

'Quiff?' Retro said.

'The squirrel. It's quite simple, I haven't been looking for you, I'm here because you have my friend who, by the way, is an honorary member of the Cat Council' I said.

Retro frowned, and shot an uncertain look at me, backing away. He shouted 'to me' and four other soggy felines I didn't recognise came out from behind the nearest trees. They ran over, encircling me. They were a similar age to Retro and I assumed they were part of V-C's.

It doesn't matter. Whether you searched, or told I was here, we will ensure everyone knows you broke your word and sought your revenge for Vincent. You'll be banned from the Council and shamed. You'll be the first, there will be others, and March won't have a Council to be an Elder to by the time we've finished' Retro sneered.

I stood my ground.

'I ... know the ... truth Quiff stuttered, his teeth chattering. He was shivering violently.

'You're not going to be alive to tell anyone' Retro yelled.

'Oh, but we all heard the canine, Connie, shouting that you had our friend Quiff; the truth is already known' a voice said behind me.

I glanced around and saw Lunar, calmly sat on the railing of the band stand. A little to the left of me, Jasper was walking towards us. Even with his wet fur plastered to his body, he has an impressive menacing presence.

Retro took advantage of my glancing at Lunar and with a scream, flung himself at me.

I was caught off balance. His claws dug into my side as he knocked me over, and pain ripped into me. I went for a Full Claw Attack to his head and neck; and made good contact. Retro screeched and backed away. I staggered to my feet as the grey and white feline hissed and lunged at me.

'Run Quiff! Go!' I yelled, and out of the corner of my eye, saw Quiff hesitate for a moment before heading to the nearest tree, chased by the ginger tabby.

I hit out at the grey and white feline with a swipe to his chest whilst he was mid-lunge, and positioned again ready to defend myself.

Retro ran at me and struck at my head, I dodged and his claw bit into my shoulder. I twisted and gave him a right paw hook. He screamed as I hit his retreating rump.

I glanced at Lunar, who had jumped off the band stand rail. She'd chased down the ginger tabby who she had pinned to the ground. Her white fur was wet and muddy but she didn't look the worse for wear. Jasper had batted two of the other cats, as if they were mere flies, and were momentarily dazed. He walked towards me, and the two other cats eyed him warily, but didn't approach.

I looked up and saw Quiff safely on a high branch. There were plenty of trees around which he could leap to and get away; I knew he was safe.

I nodded to Lunar to release the ginger who sprang up and ran to Retro.

I was breathing heavily, but I could see I'd wounded Retro as a little blood seeped into his fur. It struck me that seeing him hurt gave me no pleasure or any feeling that I'd got vengeance for Vincent.

'This isn't over; we'll be back. March's Council will end soon, and Vixen will be the Grand Elder!' Retro hissed. He turned and sprinted off with his crew towards a small tabby, who stared hard at me with narrowed orange eyes, like fire, before turning and sauntering after Retro with her tail in the air.

Chapter Fifteen

It's a bit of a blur after watching Vixen, Retro and the V-C's leave. All I can remember is Lunar and Jasper both yelling at me to keep moving, but I just wanted to lie down. My legs were wobbly and I felt very tired, wet and cold. I do recall a canine barking, and a pair of wet muddy trainers with a green tick on them appearing in my line of vision, before the sensation of being lifted. I don't just let anybody pick me up, so I know I struggled a bit before I blacked out.

All I can smell now is disinfectant. I open my eyes and blink at the bright white light shining through the mesh of the cage I'm in. I don't believe it, I'm at the Vets! I can't look, but I must, I need to check I have all my limbs. I know what the vets are like.

I decide not to look, but move my legs, one at a time, and relieved that they are all there. I should just lie still and not bring attention to myself, they'll give me something I don't want. I tried to doze, but I couldn't relax. I felt I needed to remember something important, but I couldn't think what it was, my mind felt like it was stuffed with fur. To distract myself, I moved my head slightly and looked outside the mesh.

'Hello Claude' Stilettoes said as her head appears.

She looks a bit hazy, like a Claude Monet painting. I blink, and her face sharpens into focus. She's smiling at me. Her hair is enclosed is some sort of net which is a pity as she has nice hair. She may have a nice smile and laughing kind eyes but she won't win me over.

I sniff and look away.

Stilettoes laughs and says 'Don't worry, you'll be as fit as a fiddle soon. Let's get you something to eat, that'll make you feel better and I'll call your people to collect you later.'

The offer of food got my attention. I was hungry, but what a Vet thinks is food and what I do are two entirely different things. I was presented with a dish of what I can only describe as "mush", tasteless, chew less, smelly mush. I ate it, imagining it was pilchards because I was so hungry but never, ever, ever again.

I must have dozed off because the next thing I knew, I was looking up at Anna's worried face peering down at me, her eyes dribbling with water. She held me gently in her arms. I blinked at her, feeling safe and happy and then realised that all I could see was her face, the area around her had disappeared. I sighed, as understanding hit me. I was in a cone.

Alex came out of the shop and gave me a big hug when I got home. Connie made a real fuss insisting that I rest. Vincent was just happy he had an opponent in the art of ping pong twirling and wanted to teach me.

I declined Vincent's offer, I ache in parts I didn't know I had, felt very tired and a bit deflated, like a saggy balloon. Anyone wearing a cone would feel down, it's not natural, but I wouldn't be trying to dislodge it. Instead, I'd get some sleep and when I felt like it, shoe spot from the gate to pass the time.

I spotted the medicine the Vet had given Anna. It lurked on the kitchen top next to the kettle. Since watching Vincent get better when medicine was given to him, I've realised, that the pills the Vet insist we have isn't the Vets way of making our lives a misery. It isn't Stilettoes fault medicine tastes as awful as the food at her surgery. I want the medicine. I want to feel better but, I have to be careful; I can't just accept the medicine without a fight. If I just allow Anna to give it me, without a fuss, Anna and Alex may get suspicious about my intelligence. To be honest, I haven't really got the energy, but I'll need to act normal and have the usual tussle with Alex in his oven gloves, and Anna trying to get a pill down me.

I needn't have worried. Anna is intelligent too; learning from her experience with Vincent. She served me pilchards, hiding the medicine amongst the fish. A bit did taste funny, but I ate it anyway knowing now it would do me good.

It was Tuesday afternoon and I felt sore but more myself. Vincent is having an afternoon nap on the kitchen floor, having picked a spot where the sun shone through the window. Connie, smelling like fresh air, after a long afternoon walk with Alex, lay in her sphinx pose next to me. She told me quietly that it had been Duke's upright who had picked me up. They had been running in the park and Duke spotted me lying on the ground with Lunar and Jasper sitting next to me. Duke had barked at Lunar and Jasper, who'd run away, understanding they needed to behave like cats, with the uprights perception that we are afraid of canines. I would thank Lunar, Jasper and Duke when I saw them.

My peaceful catch up with Connie was shattered when Mabel barged through the pet flap, bounced up to me, and said 'Hi Uncle Claude, how are you feeling?'

'Much better thank you' I said.

Vincent woke up, yawned, stretched, and wandered over to sit next to Mabel.

'Good, I'll report back' Mabel said.

'What do you mean, who are you reporting to?' Vincent said.

'March has asked Pickle to find out how Claude is. She's been worried about you, everyone has. Quiff wants to come and see you, but Monty says it's unlikely your uprights will want a squirrel in their home.

I nodded.

'Oh, I nearly forgot, Quiff and Lunar told the Council what happened at the park. The whisper that's going around is that March knows Retro's attack on Vincent was deliberate.'

'What do you mean?' Connie said, her eyes startled.

'I'm not really sure to be honest' Mabel said and looked at me.

I didn't either, but in the back of my clouded mind, the niggle that I'd had since waking up at the Vets, like something you can't put your paw on, began to take shape.

I finally remembered his last words to me, "Vixen will be Grand Elder." It seemed the attack on Vincent, and the knowledge that I had been ordered not to seek him out, was a plan to get me, as a Council member, to break March's orders. If I'd broken my word, I wouldn't have been able to live with myself, but it wouldn't have been good for March either. The felines in our district may start to think that she'd lost her authority and if they thought that, the felines may even decide she needed to be replaced, perhaps even with Vixen. I shuddered at the thought and Vincent looked at me wide eyed.

He knew Vincent's name too, admitting he had hurt him. Retro didn't live in the area, so he wouldn't necessarily know who Vincent was or his connection to me. I thought about the other feline Council members, Monty, Jasper, Freddie and Luna and realised that none of them lived with another thumbless being.

'Are you alright Claude, you've gone very quiet' Vincent asked.

'Yes, of course I'm fine' I said glancing at Connie who'd been watching me.

Connie nodded, understanding I'd talk to her later when we were alone.

There wasn't much chance to talk as it turned out, Anna ushered Esther into the kitchen followed by Ida Morris. Esther looked like her old self, her cheeks glowing pale pink, a twinkle in her eye and two pencils neatly securing her hair at the back of her head.

'Ida, Esther, make yourselves at home and have a seat whilst I get the kettle on' Anna said.

Ida pulled out a chair from the table and sat down. I can tell you Ida takes her Wellington boots off when indoors.

'There you are Claude; you've had us worried' Esther said as she bent over and gently stroked my back.

'It's most unlike him to get into a scrap, the Vet seems to think it was either a fox or a large cat. We did wonder if it was the same one that hurt Vincent' Anna said frowning, whilst busily making tea and placing cups, saucers, a sugar bowl, and the milk jug on the table.

Esther stroked Connie, running her hand down her long ears, and was introduced to Mabel. Vincent has never been one who likes being stroked, I think that will change but for now he hid behind Connie.

'I have some very good news' Esther said brightly.

'I thought you looked more cheerful' Anna said, sitting down at the table and pouring tea.

'Yes. I have my things back, or rather, I will have soon. They are at the police station at the moment. It turns out that young man who climbed the tree on Amble Road was one of the people who broke into my house. You were right Anna, the two crystal swans were mine, and the rest of them were with his mate, the person I painted a picture of. It turns out there were three of them, and they did run a double-glazing business; Acorn Glazing.'

'Oh Esther, that is good news' Anna said.

'It's a relief the police identified the thieves. He and his friends won't be stealing from good folk in the village, well, for a while at least' Ida said.

'It was lucky wasn't it, that Bailey chased him into the tree. I don't think the police had much to go on, without any witnesses or finding any evidence' Esther said.

'I don't think luck had much to do with it, eh Claude?' Ida said smiling at me with a twinkle in her dark brown eyes.

I'd never really looked at Ida's eyes before, I'd always been fascinated by her Wellington boots, but now I lay sphinx like mesmerised by the warmth in them.

'I'm just happy for you Esther' Anna said cheerfully.

'I am too' I said.

'Very well said Claude' Ida agreed, smiling broadly.

ABOUT THE AUTHOR

Rose Henry is a native of the beautiful county of Derbyshire, and with her husband, owned a village shop for ten years. It was an eye-opening experience but rewarding meeting some remarkable people and their pets. Rose and her husband have always lived with cats and dogs and love their quirky natures, along with the squirrels that inhabit the garden. Rose is a strong believer and supporter of animal welfare.

Printed in Great Britain
by Amazon